C

"We'll get married."

Tasha's whole body stilled. "Why?" *Because you love me?*

"It's an expedient solution," Jared replied.

She felt as if her heart tore, and then shattered into a thousand pieces. "I don't want a marriage based on *duty*."

His eyes darkened. "We're sexually compatible."

On a scale of one to ten, she'd agree that what they shared was a twenty. Mind-blowing. She hadn't experienced anything like it.

Aware she was dying inside, Tasha said, "Pregnancy wasn't part of it. Nor was marriage."

"You're carrying our child."

D1402287

She's sexy,
successful...
and
PREGNANT!

EXPECTING!

The Pregnancy Proposal
by
Helen Bianchin

Relax and enjoy our wonderfully popular series
about couples whose passion results in
pregnancies...sometimes unexpected!

We guarantee that all our characters
will fall in love with not only their new babies
but also each other, and all will discover that the
road to love is never easy, but always worth it!

Our next arrival will be

Pregnancy of Convenience (#2329)
by
Sandra Field

Available wherever Harlequin books are sold.

Helen Bianchin

THE PREGNANCY PROPOSAL

EXPECTING!

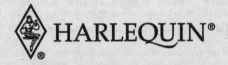

HARLEQUIN®

TORONTO • NEW YORK • LONDON
AMSTERDAM • PARIS • SYDNEY • HAMBURG
STOCKHOLM • ATHENS • TOKYO • MILAN • MADRID
PRAGUE • WARSAW • BUDAPEST • AUCKLAND

If you purchased this book without a cover you should be aware
that this book is stolen property. It was reported as "unsold and
destroyed" to the publisher, and neither the author nor the
publisher has received any payment for this "stripped book."

ISBN 0-373-12313-2

THE PREGNANCY PROPOSAL

First North American Publication 2003.

Copyright © 2003 by Helen Bianchin.

All rights reserved. Except for use in any review, the reproduction or
utilization of this work in whole or in part in any form by any electronic,
mechanical or other means, now known or hereafter invented, including
xerography, photocopying and recording, or in any information storage
or retrieval system, is forbidden without the written permission of the
publisher, Harlequin Enterprises Limited, 225 Duncan Mill Road,
Don Mills, Ontario, Canada M3B 3K9.

All characters in this book have no existence outside the imagination of
the author and have no relation whatsoever to anyone bearing the same
name or names. They are not even distantly inspired by any individual
known or unknown to the author, and all incidents are pure invention.

This edition published by arrangement with Harlequin Books S.A.

® and TM are trademarks of the publisher. Trademarks indicated with
® are registered in the United States Patent and Trademark Office, the
Canadian Trade Marks Office and in other countries.

Visit us at www.eHarlequin.com

Printed in U.S.A.

CHAPTER ONE

SURPRISE, shock, were only two of the emotions swirling inside Tasha's head as she walked from the doctor's office and slid in behind the wheel of her car.

For seemingly endless minutes she sat staring sightlessly through the windscreen as the words echoed and re-echoed inside her head.

Eight weeks pregnant.

How could she be *pregnant*, for heaven's sake?

A tiny bubble of hysterical laughter rose to the surface. She knew the *how* of it... She just didn't understand why, when she'd taken the Pill as regular as clockwork and never missed.

Nothing was infallible, the doctor had informed as he listed a few exclusions. One of which proved startlingly applicable, pinpointing a nasty gastric-flu virus that had laid her low for a few days when she hadn't been able to keep anything down.

Including the Pill, obviously. Sufficient to throw protection from conception out the window for that month.

Dear heaven. The groan was inaudible as it echoed in her mind. What was she going to do?

She was twenty-seven, a corporate lawyer. A

good one. She had a career, a partner. Her life was carefully planned...

Pregnancy wasn't on the agenda.

She closed her eyes, then opened them again.

Jared. Her heart lurched in tandem with her stomach. What would his reaction be?

One thing was sure...his surprise would match or outstrip her own.

How would he accept fatherhood?

A few differing scenarios swept through her mind, from enthusiasm and warmth, support...to the opposite end of the spectrum.

No, a silent voice screamed from deep inside. Termination was out of the question. Without thought she placed a hand to her waistline in a gesture of protective reassurance.

There could be no question this child was Jared's...but it was also *hers.* And no matter how Jared viewed its existence, she intended to have it. Life as a solo mother wouldn't be a piece of cake, but she'd manage.

What if Jared proposed marriage? Oh, sure. Pigs flew, and cows jumped over the moon!

There was little doubt he viewed their relationship as permanent...well, as permanent as any intimate liaison could be. Commitment, *sans* the sanctity of marriage.

Until now, she'd been fine with the arrangement.

Except there was a third life to consider in this equation. Decisions would need to be made. Only then would she know which direction her life would take.

Without thinking she instinctively reached into her bag and retrieved her cell-phone, only to pause as she keyed in the first digit, then disconnect the call.

Jared was due in court this afternoon, and his cell-phone would be switched through to his rooms. Any direct contact would have to wait until this evening.

Besides, this sort of news should be imparted in person, not via a telephone!

She could, she decided, plan a special candlelit dinner, dress in a provocative little number, be openly seductive during the main, then deliver the news over dessert.

But not tonight. An unladylike curse slid from her lips with the sudden realisation they were due to dine out. A Law Society soirée, one of many organised throughout the year for differing reasons.

Tasha stifled a slip into black humour at the thought of imparting her news *sotto voce* as they mixed and mingled with the city's legal scions in the foyer of the grand hotel. Perhaps she could convey the information in a seductive whisper between the soup starter and the entrée?

He might very well choke, whereupon someone would have to administer the Heimlich manoeuvre…and that would never do.

Better, perhaps, to be more circumspect. She could always call into a babywear boutique, purchase a pair of white knitted bootees and place them on his pillow. How was that for subtlety?

Tasha's mind unconsciously slid to the man who was causing her so much grief…and didn't know whether to smile or shed a few tears at the reflection.

Jared North was known as one of Brisbane's most sought-after barristers. In his late thirties, he was a brilliant man in his chosen field with the verbal skill to reduce the most hardened criminal to an insecure incoherent in the courtroom and tear the defence attorney's testimony to shreds.

She'd first met him three years ago at a dinner for the legal fraternity. His reputation preceded him, and, while she'd seen his photo in newspapers and magazines, nothing prepared her for seeing the man in the flesh.

One look across a crowded room was all it took, and her insides began to melt. Tall, broad shoulders, the way he wore his impeccably cut suit set him apart from his associates. Hewn facial features sculpted by nature's hand gifted him a strong jaw, wide cheekbones, a perfectly symmetrical nose. Muscle and skin assembled to provide almost a Latin look, a throwback it was said to his maternal Andulusian ancestry. But it was the eyes, well-set, dark and knowing as sin, that pulled a woman in. There was the promise of innate sensuality and unbridled passion beneath the sophisticated façade. And something else she recognised at a base level, but didn't care to define.

That night it was as if the room and its occupants

faded from the periphery of her vision. There was only the man, and an awareness that fizzed her blood and sent her heart racing to an accelerated beat.

He crossed the room, slowly weaving his way towards her, pausing momentarily as one associate or another sought his attention. But his gaze caught and held her own, his intention clear as she waited for him to join her.

Afterwards she had no clear recollection of their conversation. Instead, she heard only the deep timbre of his voice, an intonation that hinted at education abroad. She became fascinated by his mouth, the sensual curve of his lower lip, the warmth portrayed when he smiled.

An astute, clever and dangerous man, she perceived, instinctively aware even then he would have a profound effect on her life.

After three months of dating Jared suggested she move in with him. Tasha opted to wait six months, unwilling to leap too soon into a committed relationship where lust formed a large part of its foundation.

Now, two years down the track, they shared his luxurious apartment in one of Brisbane's prestigious inner suburbs overlooking the river.

Life was good. Better than good. They devoted a lot of time to their individual careers, and each other, socialising on occasion. There was an apartment on the Gold Coast, less than an hour's drive south, where they frequently escaped for the weekend. Sun, sand and relaxation, it provided a different lifestyle to the one they each led through the week.

At no time had *marriage* been mentioned.

Tasha didn't want it mentioned, unless it was for the right reason...*love*. The everlasting, ever-after kind.

The beep from her pager was an intrusive sound, and she reached for it, read the message to call her office, and retrieved her cell-phone.

Minutes later she fired the ignition, eased her BMW out from the medical centre car park and gained the arterial road leading into the city.

It was a glorious day, the sky a clear azure with the merest drift of cloud. Lush green lawns, late-spring flowers provided colour and there was the promise of summer in the sun's warmth.

Brisbane's city-scape loomed in the distance. Splendid architecture in varying office towers and apartment high-rises of concrete, glass and steel. The wide river was a focal scenic point, together with a university, arts centre and the bustling Southbank with its many attractions.

Within minutes Tasha turned into a private key-operated inner-city car park, then drove to her allotted space and took the lift to the fifteenth floor.

The receptionist manning the front desk resembled a model from *Vogue* magazine. An admirable reflection of the head partner's dictum professional image was everything. Amanda certainly aided that, and then some.

'Your two-thirty appointment is delayed; you have messages on your desk.'

'Thanks.' Tasha summoned a smile in acknowledgement as she passed through Reception *en route* to her office.

Work proved a necessary distraction, and she checked her appointment schedule, ensured her secretary had the requisite paperwork ready for perusal, and gave instructions for three follow-up calls.

Two client consultations and a late-afternoon meeting brought the working day to a close. Something she viewed with relief, for her powers of concentration seemed to have zoomed off to another planet.

There had been moments when she was totally focused, others when a coloured illustration of a tiny foetus from the pages of the doctor's medical book proved a haunting intrusion.

So tiny, so alive.

For a moment she stood perfectly still, consumed by a fierce protectiveness that drove out rational thought.

Then she extracted her briefcase and slid in printouts with various notations she needed to examine in preparation for a meeting tomorrow, collected her laptop, walked out to the foyer and took a lift down to the car park.

The best thing to be said about peak-hour traffic was that it moved... This evening, the speedometer didn't register a notch over ten kilometres an hour through the inner city.

Her cell-phone beeped, signalling an incoming text message, and she activated it while she sat waiting for the lights to change.

Jared... *Delayed an hour.*

Tasha wasn't sure whether to be peeved or relieved. While there was a part of her that wanted to get Jared's reaction out of the way, there was also a certain reluctance.

Neither of which made much sense, she determined as she garaged her car and rode the lift to their apartment.

Situated on a high floor, it was one of two sub-penthouses in a prestigious apartment block on the river with splendid views of the city.

Spacious with cream marble-tiled floors, large expanses of floor-to-ceiling tinted glass, there were oriental rugs, modern furniture in cream and beige, with splashes of colour provided by modern works of art adorning the walls.

The lounge and dining-room were large, the kitchen and utilities modern, and the master suite was a dream with its large bed and adjoining bathroom. Of the three remaining bedrooms, Jared had converted one into a legal reference library with a desk, computer and electronic equipment for his own use. Another room held a day bed, and a desk which Tasha could use for her own needs. The third bedroom was a guest suite.

Tasha crossed into the kitchen, extracted a bottle of juice from the refrigerator and poured some into a glass, drank some, then she sliced cheese onto a biscuit and ate it.

Over the past week or two she had seemed inclined to want to nibble food at frequent intervals. Another symptom of pregnancy?

She'd have to buy a book and study it, she perceived as she walked through to the master suite.

Choosing what to wear didn't pose too much of a problem, and she tossed an elegant black evening suit onto the bed, then made for the shower.

It was a while before she emerged and, dry, a towel wound round her slender form, she began style-drying her hair. Dark sable, it tumbled in wavy curls down onto her shoulders.

Next came make-up, and she chose subtle shadings to highlight her gold-flecked dark brown eyes, then she donned fresh underwear and entered the bedroom.

Dressed, she slid her feet into black stiletto pumps which added four inches to her petite frame.

Selecting jewellery, she was in the process of fastening a pendant at her nape when Jared walked into the room.

Her gaze met his, and her stomach fluttered at the warmth evident in those dark grey, almost black eyes.

His jacket was hooked over one shoulder, he'd loosened his tie and he'd undone the top button of his shirt and removed his cufflinks.

He bore the faint shadow of a man who needed

to shave twice a day, and it lent him a slightly dangerous air.

Lethal, she amended as she felt her body stir in recognition of her attraction to him.

Passion, even in its mildest form, had the ability to liquefy her bones. All he had to do was look at her, and she was lost.

His mouth curved into a musing smile as he crossed to her side.

'Let me fix that for you.'

He was close, much too close. She felt her body quiver as his fingers brushed her skin, and she was conscious of every breath she took, the heightened sensuality as she caught the faint aroma of his cologne, the male heat that was uniquely his.

Tasha felt his hands shift to her shoulders, the brush of his mouth against the sensitive curve at the edge of her neck.

'Beautiful.'

She caught the slight huskiness in his voice, and deliberately stepped away. 'If you don't shower and change we're going to be late.'

There was a moment's silence, then he shifted and turned her round to face him. 'Bad day?'

The query was softly voiced, and she met his narrowed gaze with equanimity.

'Something like that.'

'Want to talk about it?'

Tasha shook her head. 'We don't have time.'

Jared caught hold of her chin between thumb and forefinger, and tilted it. 'We can make time.'

No, they couldn't. This was going to take a while if she was going to do it right. And there shouldn't be any distractions or time restriction.

She knew if she said the word, he would delay their departure for as long as it took. And part of her wanted to, very much.

His presence at tonight's event was expected. Reneging without good reason was unthinkable.

She managed a faint smile. 'It can wait.'

He cast her a brooding look, unable to define much from her expression.

'Really,' she assured.

'Later.'

It was capitulation, and she released a silent sigh of relief as he tossed his jacket down onto the bed, pulled off his tie, then began to discard the rest of his clothes.

Half an hour later she slid into the passenger seat of Jared's late-model Jaguar and sat in silence as he traversed the ramp to street-level, then eased the powerful car towards the city.

She'd gained a reprieve. But only a temporary one. At evening's end, Jared would have the facts and be aware of her options.

CHAPTER TWO

THE evening's legal soirée followed the pattern of those preceding it...superb venue, tastefully decorative bite-size food offered on silver platters by an array of uniformed waitresses, while the drinks stewards hovered, presenting guests with champagne and orange juice.

It was all very elegant, Tasha observed. Dinner suits and black tie for the men were *de rigueur*, and the women excelled themselves in gowns of varying design, length and colour.

There were colleagues to greet and spend time engaging in pleasant conversation before moving on. Notable peers who were important to acknowledge.

She found it vaguely amusing to be partnered by one of the latter, aware of the difference between dignified patronage and obsequious awe as members of the legal fraternity sought Jared's attention.

Something he handled with friendly professionalism, never faltering in recalling a name or the firm for whom they worked.

'How do you do that?' Tasha asked quietly.

A slight smile curved his mouth, tilting the edges and deepening the vertical line slashing each cheek. His eyes were dark and held a musing gleam. 'Memory training.'

Something he'd honed to perfection during his law-school days. An asset that was equally lauded and feared by his contemporaries.

She selected a canapé from a proffered tray and bit into it, then took a sip from her glass...orange juice, when she would normally have chosen champagne.

Dinner was a splendid meal, the food superb, and their table companions provided interesting conversation.

There were the customary speeches, and Tasha listened attentively, aware throughout the evening she was merely acting an expected part.

If Jared noticed, he gave no sign, although there was more than one occasion when she became aware of his lingering gaze, and she caught the faintly brooding quality evident.

His presence at her side was a constant, and she was supremely conscious of him, the light touch of his hand at her waist, the warmth of his smile.

All she had to do was look at him to feel the blood pump faster through her veins, and sensation unfurl deep within. It became a fine kind of madness that was entirely sensual as heat consumed her body and liquefied her bones.

Those large hands could wreak magic to each and every pulse-beat, and his mouth... Dear heaven, even thinking about what his mouth could do wrought havoc with her senses.

Almost as if he knew, he reached for her hand and threaded his fingers through her own. His thumb-pad soothed the criss-cross of veins pulsing rapidly on the inside of her wrist, and she curled her fingers, letting the fingernails bite into his flesh a little.

Did he know what he did to her? Without doubt, she alluded wryly. She'd been *his* from the start, ensnared by the power, the sheer male magnetism that was his alone.

The question that needed to be asked...and answered, she ventured silently, was how she affected *him?* Sexually, what they shared together was good. Better than good. Earth-shattering. She'd have sworn on her life his loss of control wasn't faked.

But was it *love*...or merely lust? Sadly, she couldn't be sure.

'Let's get out of here,' Jared drawled as he pulled her close. 'The evening is just about done, and we've fulfilled our social obligation.'

His gaze narrowed fractionally as he caught the edge of weariness evident on her features, the faint shadows beneath her eyes. Dammit, she looked fragile. The onset of a virus? She'd admitted to a difficult day at the office, which was most unlike her. She excelled with challenge of any kind.

Tasha made no protest, although the thought of exchanging a social comfort zone for what would inevitably prove an explosive situation accelerated her nervous tension.

It took a while to escape, for there were certain courtesies to observe, and Tasha sat quietly in the car as Jared sent it purring through the city streets.

They entered the apartment close to midnight...the witching hour, Tasha acknowledged, and wondered at the irony of it.

'Coffee?'

'No, thanks.'

Jared closed the distance between them, and glimpsed the faint wariness evident in her gaze. He caught her chin between thumb and forefinger and tilted it.

'You've been as nervous as a cat on hot bricks all evening.' His musing drawl had an underlying edge to it. 'Why?'

There was no easy way to impart her news. She hesitated, reflecting on a few rehearsed lines she'd silently practised...in the office, driving from work, during the evening...and discarded each and every one of them.

'Tasha?' A slight smile widened his mouth. 'What did you do? Earn a traffic violation? Over-extend your credit limit?' The last was an attempt at humour, and he caught the faint roll of her eyes before she shook her head. 'No?' He brushed his thumb over her lower lip, felt its slight quiver, and ditched any further attempt to lighten the situation. 'I take it this is something serious?'

Oh, man, she reflected ruefully. You don't know the half of it.

'Do I continue to play twenty questions, or are you going to tell me?'

She threw out the soft approach and went for hard facts. 'I'm pregnant.'

Was it benefit of courtroom practice that allowed no expression to show on his features? There was no surprise or shock, and Tasha pre-empted the question she thought he'd be compelled to ask.

'I had a doctor's appointment late this morning. He confirmed it.' She spread her hands in a helpless gesture, then sought to explain how and why the Pill hadn't been effective. 'I thought I had a lingering virus.'

Of the many scenarios she'd imagined depicting his reaction, she hadn't counted on his silence.

She looked at him carefully. 'I won't consider a termination.' *This child is mine,* she cried silently. *But so much a part of you.* The thought of relinquishing its chance to life almost killed her.

Dear heaven, why didn't he say something... anything.

'Did I ask that of you?'

All afternoon and evening she'd been on tenterhooks worrying about his reaction, agonising if the existence of a child might spell the end of their relationship.

'We'll get married.'

Her whole body stilled. 'Why?' *Because you love me?*

'It's an expedient solution.'

She felt as if her heart tore, then shattered into a thousand pieces. 'I don't want a marriage based on *duty*. And I sure as hell don't want my child to be brought into a loveless arrangement.'

Jared's eyes darkened. 'Loveless?' A muscle bunched at the side of jaw. 'How can you say that?'

'Have either of us mentioned the word *love*?' He hadn't, not once. And because he hadn't, neither had she. 'We're sexually compatible.' On a scale of one to ten, she'd accord what they shared as a twenty. Mind-blowing. She hadn't experienced anything like it, and doubted she ever would with anyone else.

'We've been incredibly indulgent, with no thought to changing the relationship in any way.' She paused, aware she was dying inside. 'Pregnancy wasn't part of it. Nor was marriage.'

'You're carrying our child.'

'Marriage doesn't necessarily have to follow.'

'I'm proposing that it does.'

She held his gaze. 'Answer me honestly. If my pregnancy wasn't an issue, would you have broached the subject of marriage?'

Please give me the reassurance I want, *need*, she silently begged. Sweep away my doubts and uncertainties by saying just one word, *now*.

His expression didn't change. 'I imagine so, eventually.'

She felt as if a sword pierced her heart, and it took considerable effort to keep her voice steady. 'I don't want you as a husband out of a sense of obligation.'

'Two years together and you question my obligation?'

It wouldn't do if she crumbled at his feet. 'Two years during which either one of us has been free to walk away,' Tasha said quietly. 'My definition of marriage comprises love and a permanent "till death us do part" significance. If you had wanted that, you'd have suggested marriage before now.'

'Which you choose to interpret as me preferring an open relationship with no legal ties?'

His slight hesitation together with his choice of words had provided an answer.

'Yes.'

'And you couldn't possibly be wrong?'

Do you know how desperately I want to be wrong? She felt like railing at him. *I love you.* I want to be with you for the rest of my life...as your wife, the mother of your children. But not, dear God, as a second-best choice borne out of duty. I'd rather be alone than know I'd forced you into a role you didn't want.

'I don't think so.'

'But you're not sure?'

'Don't use counsellor tactics on me. Save them for the courtroom.'

Without a further word she turned and walked down the hall to the master bedroom where she caught up her wrap, a few essential toiletries, and made her way to the guest room. Only to come face-to-face with Jared.

She registered the suit jacket hooked over one shoulder, the loosened tie and the semi-unbuttoned shirt. It lent him a rakish look and succeeded in activating a spiral of sensation she fought to restrain.

'What do you think you're doing?' His appraisal

was swift, and his eyes darkened as she made to move past him.

'Sleeping in the spare room.'

She could sense the tension in his large body, the tightening of muscle and sinew as he exercised control. 'The hell you are.'

The deadly softness of his voice issued a warning she elected to ignore. 'I don't want to have sex with you.'

His gaze hardened, a fractional shift of his features that reminded her of a panther's stillness the moment before it leapt to attack. 'I accept that. But we share the same bed.'

And risk succumbing to his brand of subtle persuasion?

She was all too aware it would only take the glide of his hand on her hip, the familiar trail to her belly and the gentle but sure fingers seeking the soft folds at the juncture of her thighs to rouse her into semi-wakefulness and turn to him in the night.

By the time she remembered, it would be too late, and she'd be lost. 'I don't think so.'

'Tasha—'

'Don't.' She lifted a hand, then let it fall to her side. 'Please,' she added. 'I want to be alone right now.'

It was the *please* that got to him.

'We need to talk.'

'We've already done that.' Her voice was even, calm, when inside she was breaking apart. Hurting so badly, so deeply, she'd probably bear the scars from it for the rest of her life.

His gaze locked with hers, the force of his will vying with her own for long, timeless seconds, then he moved aside to let her pass.

The guest room held its own linen closet, and she undressed, donned her wrap, removed her make-up, then she made up the bed, slid between the cool percale sheets and switched off the bedlamp.

Sleep came easily, but she woke in the early hours of the morning, momentarily disoriented by her surroundings until she remembered where she was and why.

The bed was comfortable, but she wasn't curled in against Jared's muscled frame as he held her close, even in sleep. She missed the steady beat of his heart, his reassuring warmth. The way he seemed to sense when she stirred during the night, how he'd gather her in and press his lips to the curve of her shoulder.

Inevitably it would lead to lovemaking, and she delighted in the fact he could never get enough of her. Secure in the relationship and what they shared.

Not any more, a tiny voice taunted. You blew it.

It was then the tears began to well, spilling over to slip in slow rivulets to her temples and become lost in her hair.

Tasha lay awake, staring at the darkened ceiling until the grey light of an early dawn crept between the shutters, giving the room shape and form, followed by subtle shades of colour.

It was too soon to rise and meet the day, and any further hope of sleep was out of the question. She could slip into the master suite and retrieve what she needed to wear into the office. Except she'd encounter Jared...something that was unavoidable, but she'd prefer to face him when they were both dressed. Which meant she'd need to wait until six-thirty, when he left the apartment for his daily workout in the downstairs gym.

At six-forty she took a leisurely shower in the hope it would ease the tiredness. It didn't, and she brushed her hair until her scalp tingled.

With care she tidied the bed, caught up the clothes she'd worn the previous evening, and entered the master suite.

The large bed bore witness of Jared's occupation, the covers a tangled mess, the pillows bunched at different angles. So he hadn't had an easy night of it, either.

Somehow the thought gave her pleasure as she crossed to the large walk-in wardrobe.

Clothes were everything, and she began with her sexiest underwear, pulled on the sheerest tights, added a new suit she'd bought only the week before but hadn't worn, and slid her feet into killer stiletto-heeled shoes. Then she collected her bag of cosmetics and returned down the hall to the guest suite.

Make-up was both an art form and a weapon, and she took extra care with its application, highlighting her eyes before sweeping her hair into a smooth chignon. A touch of perfume, and she was about as

ready as she'd ever be to face whatever the day
might bring.

Any hope of escaping the apartment before
Jared's return died as she entered the kitchen and
saw him seated at the breakfast table sipping black
coffee as he scanned the morning's newspaper.

His usual routine on return from the gym was to
shower, shave, dress, eat, then leave for the city.

This morning he'd chosen to reverse the process,
and the sight of him in sweats, his hair ruffled from
exertion, and looking incredibly *physical* sent the
blood racing through her veins.

He lifted his head and his gaze seared hers. It
gave him no pleasure to see the carefully masked
signs showing she hadn't slept any better than he
had.

'Coffee's hot.'

Tasha made tea, added milk, slid bread into the
toaster, then peeled and ate a banana as she waited
for the toast to pop. When it did, she spread honey,
and carried both tea and toast to the table.

Begin as you mean to go on, she bade silently.
Anything less is a compromise you don't want to
make.

'I'll arrange an apartment of my own within the
next few days,' she said quietly. She took a deep
breath, then released it slowly. Her throat felt as if
it were closing over, and she swallowed in an attempt to ease the restriction.

'You think I'll allow you to do that?' His voice
was quiet, much too quiet.

She was willing to swear she stopped breathing, and for a few timeless seconds she wasn't capable of summoning a coherent word.

'It's not your decision to make,' she managed at last.

'No?' The silky tone held something she didn't care to define.

'My child, my body.' It was as if she was hell-bent on treading a path to self-destruction.

'Our child,' he corrected. 'Our decision.' He stood to his feet, aware he outmatched her in height, size and weight. He caught the faint flicker of alarm in her eyes and derived satisfaction from it. Dammit, he'd take any advantage he could get.

She stood her ground. 'I've already made my decision.'

'Change it.'

She checked her watch. 'I have to leave, or I'll be late.' She collected her briefcase and walked from the apartment, then she took the lift down to the basement car park, slid into the BMW and sent it up to street-level.

Focusing on work took all her concentration, and it didn't sit well when a para-legal pointed out something she'd missed, when she should have picked up on it. A minor error, but it gave her pause for thought.

Tasha's lunch was a sandwich she sent out for, which she ate at her desk in between contacting real-estate agents. The sooner she tied up a lease on an apartment the better, and she made appointments to view at the end of her working day.

The afternoon didn't fare much better, and it was a relief to join the building's general exodus shortly after five.

Her first appointment didn't work out. She could have ignored the female agent's over-the-top presentation if the apartment had lived up to expectations. It didn't, and what was more the rental was way overpriced.

The second was an improvement, but Tasha didn't like the location.

'I can get you anything you want if you're prepared to pay,' the agent snapped. 'Both apartments I've shown you are in the price-range you quoted.'

'I have a few others to see tomorrow,' she dismissed coolly. 'I'll get back to you.'

Going home held a new connotation. She was very aware the apartment and everything in it belonged to Jared. Clothes and select items of jewellery comprised her possessions. She'd given up a lease on her own apartment and her furniture had been put in storage when she'd moved in with Jared.

The muted ring of her cell-phone sounded from inside her bag, and she retrieved it, checked the caller ID and felt her stomach muscles tighten. Jared.

'Where in hell are you?'

'Three blocks away at a set of traffic lights,' she answered reasonably.

'It's almost seven. You didn't think to call and say you'd be late?'

'I lost track of time.' The lights changed and cars up front began to move. 'Got to go.' She cut the connection before he had a chance to respond.

Jared was standing in the lounge, hands thrust into his trouser pockets, when she entered the apartment. The adopted casual stance belied the tense set of his features.

'Perhaps you'd care to explain?'

There was nothing like the truth. 'I was viewing apartments with an agent.' She began loosening the buttons on her jacket, only to pause part-way when she remembered all she wore beneath it was a bra…a very skimpy number that was little more than a scrap of moulded red lace.

Tasha saw his eyes flare, then harden as she re-fastened the buttons.

'A useless exercise. You're not going anywhere.'

Calm. All she needed to do was to remain calm. 'I don't believe you have the right to tell me what I can or can't do.'

Jared lifted an arm and indicated the room. 'Why move out when we can share this apartment?'

See you every morning, every night? Separate bedrooms, separate meals, polite conversation? And die a little every time? 'I don't think so,' she responded with a politeness that belied her emotions.

'Tasha.' His voice held a silky warning she chose to ignore, and her expression held a mix of fearless pride.

'I have no intention of denying you access,' she managed quietly.

'To you?'

She didn't misunderstand his implication. 'To the child,' she elaborated.

'Unlimited time. Your place or mine, but I don't get to stay?'

'I don't want the child to sense its father might only be a temporary entity who might choose to walk out of its life at any time.'

His gaze hardened measurably. 'You must know I would never do that.'

'Perhaps not.' She waited a beat. 'However, your future wife may not be so keen to welcome a child from a previous relationship.'

'As you will be my wife, that doesn't apply.'

One fine eyebrow arched in silent query. 'Another proposal you expect me to accept, when I know that, had it not been for the child, marriage was never your intention? Thanks, but no, thanks.'

A muscle tensed at the edge of his jaw. 'I don't recall saying marriage wasn't my intention.'

He was good, very good. But wasn't it the skill of his chosen profession to utilise words to their best advantage? To confuse the defendant and cleverly persuade admissions which otherwise might be withheld?

'You didn't need to.'

'You're being ridiculously stubborn.'

'Am I?' She drew in a short breath and released it. 'I guess that's my prerogative.' It took considerable courage to hold his gaze. 'If you'll excuse me, I need to go freshen up.' She checked her watch, and grimaced ruefully. 'I'm already late.'

'Late for what?'

Jared's voice held an ominous thread she chose to ignore. 'Eloise rang to say Simon is out of town for a few days, and I suggested we meet for dinner.'

'A girls' night out?'

'Yes.' She moved past him and entered the bedroom she'd occupied the night before. It didn't take long to freshen up, repair her make-up and re-do her hair.

Jared watched her emerge into the lounge, and experienced the familiar surge of desire. She was everything he wanted, all he needed. Dammit, she was *his*.

The thought of any other man coming near her...worse, being given the right, almost undid him.

Did she have any conception of how he'd managed to get through the day without seriously impairing his reputation?

'Tasha.'

She turned as she reached the door, watchful as he closed the distance between them. 'Yes?'

'You forgot something.'

A puzzled frown creased her forehead. Purse, keys... 'I don't think so.'

'This,' he murmured as he cupped a hand to her face and brushed his lips to her own, lingered, then he deepened the kiss to something warmly evocative before lifting his head.

He smiled faintly at her slight confusion, aware of her response for an unguarded instant. 'Drive carefully.'

Oh, God, she agonised as she rode the lift down to the basement car park. Why did he have to do that? She could still feel the slow sweep of his tongue on her own, the pressure of his mouth. Not to mention the quickened beat of her heart.

She made a quick call to Eloise from her cellphone to say she was running late, then she drove the car to street-level.

Traffic was heavy, with a number of vehicles heading for the city, and it was almost eight when she entered the restaurant.

'I'm so sorry,' Tasha offered as she slid into the seat opposite Eloise.

The attractive blonde smiled and indicated her half-empty glass of wine. 'A gentleman had the waiter bring me champagne with his compliments. And a note offering his—er—services for the evening.'

'Naturally you declined.'

'It was tempting,' Eloise relayed solemnly, and Tasha bit back a mischievous laugh. She'd known Eloise since their pre-teen years when they'd commiserated over pimples, teeth braces, and lusted after the male television and movie stars of the moment.

Relationships, they'd experienced a few, and supported each other when they fell apart. Now Eloise was happily married to Simon, and Tasha was with Jared...and pregnant.

Tasha picked up the menu. 'OK, what are we eating?'

The drinks waiter arrived, and she requested chilled mineral water.

'I'm driving.' It was a weak excuse, and she knew it.

'So am I,' Eloise stated. 'But one glass won't pitch either of us over the legal limit.'

They ordered, choosing an entrée, skipped the main, and settled on fresh fruit, cheese and crackers instead of dessert.

'It's no fun being virtuous.'

Tasha sipped from her glass, then replaced it onto the table. 'Speak for yourself.'

'I thought Jared might have been with you.'

'Disappointed?'

'Not in the least. We rarely get to go out on our own.'

'Without the men of the moment.'

'OK, what gives?'

Tasha picked up her glass and took a leisurely sip. 'What makes you think anything does?'

'Too many years of friendship. Are you going to talk, or do we continue to pretend nothing's wrong?'

Eloise would know soon enough, so it might as well be now. 'I'm pregnant.'

'You're kidding me.'

'I wish.'

'What do you mean, *you wish*? Maybe the timing isn't right, but Tasha…a baby. I think it's wonderful.' She leaned forward. 'So when's the wedding?'

'There isn't going to be one.'

'Excuse me?'

'I'm not going to marry Jared.'

'This is serious stuff.' Eloise pushed her plate to one side and leaned forward. 'Didn't he ask you?'

'Yes.'

'And you refused? Are you insane?'

Quite possibly. 'I don't want marriage just because it serves a purpose.'

'Stubborn,' Eloise declared with brutal honesty. 'You're being ridiculously, pathetically stubborn.'

'*Stubborn,* huh?'

'Forget the dream, and go with reality. Marry the man.'

'Sure,' Tasha agreed. 'And wonder if it'll last? If he'll be enticed by the excitement of an affair…singular or plural. Consign the wife and child to one side and indulge in extramarital sex.'

'Many marriages exist and survive in those circumstances.'

'More fool the wives who condone them.'

'You'd be surprised how many do.'

'In exchange for the mansion, social and professional status, overseas trips…not to mention their husband's wealth,' Tasha concluded cynically.

'Better the legal advantage of wife, than mistress.'

'So…why not me? Is that what you're saying?'

'What will change?' Eloise demanded. 'You

adore the guy, he clearly adores you. Dammit, you've lived together for two years. So, the pregnancy wasn't planned. So what? It happened, and it can't be undone. Well, it can, but, knowing you, you wouldn't consider abortion as an option.'

'No.'

'You'll deny your child a live-in father and the stable relationship of two full-time parents...because of stubborn pride?'

'You don't understand.'

'Take a reality check, Tasha.'

'You didn't settle for anything less than love.'

'If you remember, it was a rocky path to the altar.'

Rocky was an understatement, she reflected. An engagement that was more *off* than *on*. Yet Eloise and Simon had resolved their differences, and as far as she could tell the magic that had shimmered beneath the surface was still there.

'So you think I'm being a fool?'

'Yes.'

There was nothing like the honesty given from the benefit of a long friendship! 'Yet you know I'm going to do it my way, regardless?'

'I don't have the slightest doubt.'

Minutes later another waiter presented them with a tastefully decorated platter of fresh fruit, assorted nuts, cheese and crackers.

'Enough about me,' Tasha dismissed as the waiter took their order for tea and coffee. 'How's business?' Eloise was a high-flying executive in a public-relations firm who dealt with an interesting range of clients.

'Hectic.' The attractive blonde grimaced slightly. 'Simon's flight arrives from Tokyo an hour before mine departs for Sydney.' She rolled her eyes. 'We'll be lucky if we catch sight of each other. There's a lot to be said for the nine-to-five daily grind.'

'As opposed to fame and fortune?' Simon dealt in corporate real estate, worldwide, setting up multi-million-dollar deals involving buildings, hotels. Formerly based in New York, he'd made his home in Brisbane following his marriage to Eloise.

'I guess it would be selfish to want both?'

'Not possible,' Tasha opined solemnly.

'Because there's no such thing as a perfect world?'

'Something like that.'

It was almost eleven when they left the restaurant. The adjacent parking area was well-lit, and Eloise's car occupied the bay next to her own.

'I'll be in touch,' Eloise promised as she unlocked her door. 'Take care, Tasha, and think about what I said.'

'Shall do.'

The possibility Eloise was right didn't escape her as she followed her friend's car onto street-level.

It was a beautiful night, the sky a deep indigo sprinkled with stars and a sickle moon. Bright lights, colourful neon, traffic. Reflections of the sky-scape evident in the smooth waters of the city river.

Self-castigation was not an uplifting experience, Tasha determined as she took the exit lane from the bridge.

What was wrong with her? Why not accept Jared's proposal, enjoy being Mrs Jared North, gift her child legitimacy, and to hell with her high ideals?

She needed her head read. Anyone else would go eagerly into the marriage and be content with whatever Jared offered. She knew he cared for her. So what if lust was a poor substitute for *love*?

Any number of women would be willing to settle for less, given Jared's personal wealth, professional and social status. He was a generous man, in bed and out of it. Wasn't that *enough*?

Was she a fool for wanting it all?

The answer had to be an unequivocal *yes*.

CHAPTER THREE

THE apartment was quiet as she entered the foyer, and she crossed to the kitchen, withdrew bottled water from the refrigerator and filled a glass, drank some, then she made for the hallway.

Was Jared home?

The sudden thought he might have gone out resulted in a frown. He would have rung, surely? Or at least left a text message on her cell-phone.

'Enjoy your evening?'

He stood framed in the aperture leading to the room he used as a study. One wall was lined floor to ceiling with bookshelves, another wall contained a long credenza. There was an antique desk which held his laptop surrounded by legal files, and a thick yellow legal pad.

Attired in black jeans, a white chambray shirt unbuttoned at the neck with the sleeve cuffs carelessly turned back, his hair slightly ruffled as if he'd dragged his fingers through it, he looked vaguely piratical, even satanical.

Dark eyes, dark hair, olive skin, his expression unfathomable as he stood regarding her.

Tasha felt vaguely defensive, even wary. Normally she'd have moved in close, reached up and kissed him, sure of her welcome, the feel of his arms closing around her slender form as they pulled her in and he deepened the kiss.

Sometimes they'd talk, but most often he'd simply sweep an arm beneath her knees and carry her into their bedroom. Fast and furious, slow and gentle…one would inevitably follow the other in a long loving far into the night. Often the talking waited until morning as they showered together, ate breakfast, dressed for the day.

Now Tasha remained still, unfamiliar uncertainty meshing with an undeniable sexual attraction. 'Yes.'

Jared didn't move, and she contemplated walking straight past him to the spare bedroom.

Except there was a waiting, *watching* quality to his stance. A silent warning she instinctively knew she'd do well to heed.

'Working hard?' It was a light query, and unnecessary. He was one of a few people she knew who could survive on four or five hours' sleep and face whatever the day held with energy and purpose.

Razor-sharp was a superlative often used in reference to Jared North's mind power, his memory recall. Very little, if anything, escaped him.

'A few more hours should do it.'

The faint drawling quality sent prickles of unease up her spine. They were both being excruciatingly polite. Too polite, she perceived, aware there was a degree of anger beneath the surface of his control.

With her? Of course with her! The pregnancy was her fault. Well, not entirely, but she could have, *should* have been aware of the consequences and ensured extra precautions were taken. Except she hadn't given the possibility of pregnancy a thought.

Divine intervention? A *test* by the Deity to determine the strength of their relationship?

Oh, dammit, Tasha cursed silently. She was really losing it!

'Goodnight.' She made to step past him, only to pause as his hand closed over her shoulder. Firm fingers cupped her chin, tilting it so she had no choice but to meet his gaze. 'Don't.' Dear heaven, he was so close, too close. 'Please,' she added quietly.

Jared touched a finger to her lower lip, and he offered a faint smile. 'Afraid, Tasha?'

'Of you? No.'

'So brave.' His voice held a mocking tinge she chose to ignore.

It took courage to project *cool* when her pulse felt as if it was jumping out of her skin. 'Is there a purpose to this?'

'Does there need to be one?'

'Yes,' she managed evenly.

'By all means...' His mouth closed over hers in a gentle exploration, teasing, evocative, as he held her there.

For an instant she began to respond, the instinctive inclination automatic, then reaction set in and she strained against him, unsure whether to feel relieved or disappointed as he let her go.

'You don't play fair.' Her breath hitched a little as she sought control.

'Did you imagine I would?'

She looked at him, caught the stillness in that dark gaze, and recognised the need to act with her head and not her heart.

'No.' Beneath the sophisticated façade there was a primitive ruthlessness apparent, a hard strength coupled with indomitable power. Characteristics that made him a man feared in a court of law...and out of it.

A sensual man, she added silently, practised in the art of lovemaking and pleasing a woman. Intense passion and great *tendresse*...he employed both with considerable skill. Yet there was also the hint of sweet savagery, well-leashed, but exigent none the less.

A tiny shiver slithered the length of her spine. Jared North was someone no one in their right mind would choose to have as an enemy in any arena.

'I'm going to bed.' She turned away from him and took the few steps necessary to bring her level with the spare bedroom.

'Sleep well.'

Tasha ignored the faint irony in his voice, and chose not to respond as she entered the room. She turned on the light switch, then closed the door quietly behind her and stood leaning against it for several minutes.

She was tired, mentally, emotionally, physically, but she doubted her ability to enjoy an easy night's sleep.

There were too many thoughts chasing contrarily

through her mind, and she endeavoured to dispense with them as she removed her clothes. Make-up came next, then she donned a nightshirt and slid in between the sheets.

She must have slept, for she was caught up in a dream so realistically vivid she was *there*, living the fight to save her baby from being taken away. She screamed at the nurse to bring him back, but no sound came out, and she screamed again, louder this time, forcing her voice in a bid to be heard. But the nurse kept walking, and Tasha tried to get out of bed to go after her, only she was hooked up to various machines, drips, and she began pulling at the tubes, swearing at her seeming inability to disconnect them as she sought to free herself.

Then there was a familiar voice, hands whose soothing touch provided a calming influence, and although she heard the words, none of them seemed to register. The scene switched to another, one where the baby was now a young toddler, laughing as he played with toys on the lawn out back of a beautiful home, and she was there, watching with maternal pride.

Dreams, fantasy, wishful thinking. Perhaps a little of each. When she woke she retained a vivid recollection, and there was an awareness of the dawn filtering through the shutters, followed by the knowledge this wasn't the spare bedroom, nor was she alone.

Had she cried through the night? Or had Jared—?

'You called my name.' He'd hit the floor running

at the first scream, and arrived to pull her into his arms as the next scream emerged from her throat.

The tortured voice had chilled him to the bone, and he'd pulled her close, soothing until she quietened, then he'd brought her into his bed, gathered her in and held her through the night.

Was she aware she'd clung to him in her sleep? Whimpered indistinctly whenever he sought to ease her into a more comfortable position?

Tasha felt the strong, steady beat of his heart beneath her cheek, sensed the warmth and slight muskiness of his skin, and experienced a familiar sensation unfurling deep within. The quickened pulsebeat, the sensitised pores, and an electrifying awareness that curled through her body, rendering it boneless, *his,* anticipating the drift of his fingers, the touch of his lips.

It was an achingly familiar pattern most mornings as they indulged in a slow lovemaking. Soft sighs, lingering kisses, and the sweet sorcery of seduction.

Then they'd slip from this large bed, share a leisurely shower before dressing for the day ahead, eat breakfast together and take the lift down to the basement car park.

This morning was different. So much had changed in the past forty-eight hours. Gone was the easy camaraderie, the sanctuary of unreserved loving. Now there were barriers, doubts, reservations.

Insecurities and unresolved resentment, she added silently, aware that every second she remained quiescent related to an invitation she was reluctant to offer.

Two years of unrestrained loving, yet at this moment she felt as nervous as she had the first time they'd shared sex.

'I must get up.'

Jared's hand slid from her ribcage to her stomach. 'Stay.'

The breath caught in her throat, and she tamped down the need. If she stayed, there could only be one end, and although she craved the wild, primitive pleasure his touch would provide, she'd only despise herself afterwards for giving in.

'I can't.'

There was a lost, almost forlorn edge to her voice that tore at him more than the words she uttered.

'Stay,' he repeated gently. 'With me.'

Did he have any idea how hard it was for her to refuse? Or how easy it would be to give in? But what price a love that wasn't equal? Self-survival had to be her ultimate goal. And she couldn't, wouldn't settle for anything less than his total commitment. Willingly given, not out of duty.

Right now she needed to get out of this bed and put some distance between them, for if he kissed her she'd be lost.

'I need to go into the office early this morning.' Even as she uttered the words she was easing away from him, smooth, deliberate movements he made no effort to still as she slid from the bed and crossed to the door. If she chose to shower in the adjacent *en suite* he might see it as an invitation to join her, and the resulting intimacy would be more than she could bear.

Half an hour later she'd showered and utilised the hair-drier. All her clothes, she qualified with a faint grimace, were in the master bedroom, along with her lingerie, hose, shoes.

With luck, Jared would be in the shower and she could retrieve what she needed without him being aware she was there.

Chance would be a fine thing, she acknowledged on re-entering the bedroom. He was in the process of dressing, a pair of black silk briefs sparing his tall muscular frame from nudity.

She caught a glimpse of broad shoulders, lightly tanned flesh and the fluid movement of muscle and sinew as he reached for a white cotton shirt, aware of the ease with which he closed the buttons before pulling on elegantly tailored trousers to his waist and deftly sliding the zip fastener closed.

There was nothing she could do to prevent the spiralling sensation curling through her body. Trying to stop it was akin to halting an incoming tide…impossible.

Part of her ached for the loss of their affectionate humour, the light-hearted teasing. A week ago she'd have crossed to his side, lifted her face to his and kissed him, exulting in the lingering afterglow of a fine loving.

She adored the sight and the feel of him, his male muskiness, the subtle aroma of his favoured Cerruti cologne. It felt so right to sink into him, so incredibly reassuring to have his arms close around her slender frame and pull her in.

His mouth… Dear heaven, just thinking about the erotic pleasure he could bestow heated her blood and sent it coursing through her veins.

Stop it. The self-admonition came as a silent scream.

Tasha drew in a deep breath, then systematically gathered what she needed and retreated to the spare bedroom.

It took determined effort to dress, fix her hair and apply make-up. Force of habit had her tidying the room, straightening bedcovers, then she collected her briefcase and walked out to the kitchen where the smell of freshly perked coffee teased her taste buds.

She'd have killed for a cup of hot black coffee, and bit her lip as she filled the electric kettle, slotted bread into the toaster, and settled for tea.

'Anything in particular on the day's agenda?' Jared queried as she took a seat at the breakfast bar. 'You expressed a need to go in to work early,' he added at her faintly startled glance.

He was adept at interpreting body language, and hers held a transparent quality lacking in artifice. Infectious wit, unerring courage and conviction, honesty, integrity. Add charm, and she'd shone like a beacon in a sea of multi-layered women whose true personality lay buried so deep he'd treated them as they regarded him...a pleasant social and sexual partner.

Until Tasha.

'A few things I need to catch up on,' she managed evenly. It was an extension of the truth, for all it entailed was checking a file, making a notation, and requesting one of the stenographers insert the correction and run another copy off ready for the client to sign.

Five minutes...ten, at the most. And the client's appointment was timed for nine-thirty.

She finished her toast, drank the last of her tea, then she stood to her feet and caught up her briefcase.

'I could be late tonight.'

Jared regarded her steadily. 'Same goes. Don't wait dinner.' He reached out a hand and caught hold of her arm. 'Aren't you forgetting something?'

He took advantage of her surprise to pull her close, slanting his mouth over hers before she had a chance to resist.

She possessed the sweetest lips, full and generously curved, and he savoured them gently, nibbling at the lower centre before deepening the kiss into something flagrantly sensual.

Tasha didn't want to respond, and for the space of a few seconds she succeeded, only to succumb to the witching magic of his touch.

When he lifted his head she barely resisted the temptation to pull his head down to hers and kiss him back.

Did he sense her indecision? Perhaps deliberately playing on it in the hope it might persuade her to cease looking for an apartment of her own?

All the more reason, she determined, to seek independence. *Soon.* For the longer she remained in Jared's apartment, the harder it would be not to succumb to temptation.

Jared was a master when it came to seduction technique, she acknowledged wryly. His brooding look with its element of heat and passion, the light tracery as his fingers sought the veins at her wrist, a sensuous curve to his mouth…it added up to a magnetic culmination of the senses, and she became lost, drawn to him as a moth to a flame.

She didn't want to crash and burn. She needed to survive.

Without a word she turned and walked through the lounge to the front door, closed it quietly behind her and summoned the lift.

It became a day where anything that could go wrong, did. Two stenographers called in sick, and redistributing their workload meant documentation which should have been ready for client signature wasn't available for scheduled appointments.

Tasha's immediate superior succumbed to a migraine mid-morning and took a cab home, leaving Tasha to reshuffle appointments.

Lunch was something she sent out for and ate at her desk while she put one call after another through to various real-estate agents in the hope one of them might at least have two suitable apartments on their books she could arrange to view. Preferably after work today.

The sooner she moved into an apartment of her own the better. It was one thing if her subconscious mind was intent on providing her with nightmarish dreams...but quite another if it led to her calling Jared's name in her sleep.

A tremor ran through her body. Waking in his arms put her far too close to the danger zone.

Did he have any conception just how vulnerable she was? Or how difficult it had been not to reach for him and slip easily into their customary early-morning loving?

She'd managed to escape this morning. But how long would it take for her to give in? Especially when Jared was intent on taking unfair advantage of every situation? A day, two, *three*? Then she'd be lost, her bid for independence a foolish quirk so easily overcome. Worse, it would be at variance with her own inestimable code regarding marriage.

A pain pierced her heart, and an incredible sadness clouded her eyes. Marriage to Jared would be heaven on earth. He was her love, the very air she breathed. But she didn't want a 'comfortable' union, one based on duty or convenience.

Nor could she bear to think he felt trapped into doing the *honourable* thing because of the existence of a child.

Others had maintained a live-in relationship and raised children without the benefit of wedlock. But it went against her principles to condone a lack of total commitment to the child.

If marriage born out of love wasn't on the agenda, then it was better to bring a child into the world where clear boundaries were in place. No false misconceptions or misunderstandings from the onset.

'You have?' Tasha queried with relief, and made a note of an address, satisfied she knew the area reasonably well. 'Shall we say six-thirty?'

She disconnected the call. Two agents, each with two apartments immediately available, one of which sounded promising.

It was after five when she left the office, and she met the first agent outside the designated address.

She'd been specific with her requirements, and this didn't come close. It was a walk-up, no lift, no garage facilities. The second apartment was little better.

Two down and two to go, Tasha concluded wryly as she pulled in to where she was to meet the second agent.

The location was fine, the apartment building multi-storeyed and modern. It looked promising, she decided as she walked towards the entrance.

Half an hour later she'd signed a lease, handed over a cheque, arranged to collect a key the next day and move in on Saturday.

It was, she assured silently as she entered the stream of traffic heading towards a bridge crossing the river, a sensible decision.

So why did she feel as if she was about to amputate a limb?

Life was all about adapting to change, she qualified. This latest change would work out. She'd make sure of it.

Tasha began making a mental list. Ring a carrier and organise a time for her furniture to be collected from the storage shed and delivered to her new address. She'd need to organise utilities, the phone and electricity, shopping...

It was a relief to see Jared's car absent from his parking bay, and she rode the lift, entered the apartment, and paused long enough to make a light meal, eat it, then she discarded the office suit, took a shower, donned a robe, then she settled down at the dining-room table with her laptop.

Organisational skills were a prerequisite in any professional arena, and Tasha had serious respect for her work and the firm's clientele. Her salary package was commensurate with her qualifications and experience. Diligent dedication was an innate quality she hoped would eventually elevate her to an associate position. A partnership offer would be the ultimate.

An achiever had been a commendable tag on her scholastic report cards, a compliment from law lecturers, her legal superiors.

Becoming a single mother and taking responsibility for the rearing and education of her child shouldn't alter her goal. A number of successful women managed to rear children and uphold a career...and so would she.

There were professional nannies, childcare centres, after-school care. Boarding-school was a possibility...but not before the age of twelve. She'd share the child with Jared at alternate weekends, and arrange to split her annual leave to coincide with school holidays.

It should, Tasha decided, all work out.

She placed a hand to her waist and rested it there. An instinctive movement as she pondered the sex of her child, its precise size...and made a note to buy a book on pregnancy.

Meanwhile, she had work, and she turned her attention back to the laptop screen.

It was there Jared found her, two law books open to one side, a yellow legal pad with filled pages folded over the spine, and her appointment diary. An empty teacup rested strategically on its saucer in the mix.

'Still at it?'

Tasha lifted her head long enough to spare him a glance, then continued keying in data. 'Yes.'

He crossed into the kitchen, took a carton of milk from the refrigerator, caught up a glass, filled it, then drank long and deep.

'Tough day?' She looked pale, and her eyes seemed too large and much too dark. He stifled the urge to cross to her side, press the *save* key, shut the laptop, then sweep her into his arms and carry her to their bed.

Two nights ago he would have done precisely that, stifled her protest with a kiss, removed his clothes, disrobed her, then indulged them both in a leisurely, evocative loving.

'You don't want to know,' Tasha conceded, without glancing in his direction. She didn't need to, for her concentration was shot to hell with his presence. Looking at him would only make things worse.

'You should be resting.'

Now she did lift her head to spare him a quick look. 'What century are you in...the nineteenth?'

He moved to where she sat, aware how the silk robe shaped her breasts, glimpsed the valley between each, the soft cleavage revealed by the loosened lapels, and controlled the urge to stand behind her and loosen the silken folds even further. He knew the feel of her breasts, their firmness, the way the rosy tips peaked and hardened at his slightest touch.

Instead, he contented himself with working the pins free from the twist of hair she'd secured half-heartedly on top of her head hours before. In serious danger of falling apart, wisps had already escaped and fell in soft curls at her temples, behind her ears, at her nape.

It was a beguiling picture, and one he was unable to resist.

'Don't—please,' she added on a slightly breathless note, hating the vulnerability evident in her voice.

He let his hands linger at the curve of her nape,

then he slowly slid them to curl over each shoulder, cupping them momentarily before letting his hands drop to his sides.

'It's late, Tasha.' His voice was quiet, with a hint of gentleness. 'Pack it in, and come to bed.'

With him? As if.

Should she tell him she wanted to work until she was bone weary so she'd fall into such a deep sleep no dreams would penetrate her subconscious mind?

'Five, maybe ten minutes, then I'll be done.'

Jared shrugged out of his jacket and hooked it over one shoulder. 'I'll take a shower.'

How long would it take him to come looking for her when she didn't show? Or would he bother?

There was no precedent, dammit. In two years they'd never let their differences last through until morning. Hell, apart from the few occasions Jared had been away on business, last night was the first time they'd slept in separate beds.

Surely he didn't—couldn't, think she'd choose to ignore their argument and change her mind about moving out? That all it would take was some time, patience and understanding on his part for her to come to her senses?

If so, he was in for a rude shock.

Tasha spared her watch a glance and saw it was after eleven. Enough, she decided, was enough. Tomorrow was another day.

Minutes later she'd bookmarked her notes, restored the law books to Jared's library, and was safely ensconced in the spare bedroom.

If he came looking for her... Well, she'd deal with it, she decided as she plumped the pillow and reached out to snap off the bedside lamp.

Sleep came quickly. So quickly she was unaware of the door opening, or the shaft of light illuminating part of the room.

Jared crossed to the bed and stood looking down at her, seeing the soft features in repose, the way her hair curled against one cheek and spilled onto the pillow. One hand lay tucked beneath its edge, and she bore the innocence of a child.

Something twisted inside his gut. *His*. His woman. Stubborn, independent, and proud. He wouldn't lose her. Damned if he would.

He wanted to slip in beside her and hold her close through the night. To wake her in the early dawn light and have her reach for him.

For a long time he stood watching her, and then he turned and walked quietly from the room.

CHAPTER FOUR

JARED left early for the city, preferring quiet, uninterrupted time his chambers provided to go over the transcripts, and direct his line of questioning. He left a note for Tasha propped against the toaster, penned in the black ink he preferred.

The trial was proving to be a long, arduous one, the witnesses many, and the prosecuting attorney an arch rival who loved to grandstand the jury. A show pony, Jared acknowledged, with few, if any, scruples, walking the fine edge of the law and invoking judicial warnings as he tried the presiding judge's patience to its limit.

Yesterday's session had presented a chink… granted, only small, and probably insignificant. But he wanted the opportunity to peruse every detail.

The city was quiet at this hour, the traffic minimal, and the sky was a clear azure, the air crisp with the promise of another fine early-summer day. The river resembled mirrored glass, reflecting the tall city towers of steel and glass.

The traffic lights were mostly in his favour, and he turned in to the private car park beneath his office block, inserted his security-coded card to gain access, then swept down to his allotted parking bay.

Allowing time for a consult with his client's solicitor prior to leaving chambers, he had three hours before he needed to gown up and head off to court.

The lift transported him with electronic speed to a high floor, and he entered the large foyer with its empty secretarial station. He savoured the silence and the solitude as he crossed to his rooms and unlocked the door.

From that moment he assumed another persona, giving everything over to the case in hand, its nuances, flaws, the jury's perception of them, and how he could tailor his queries, his address, to maximum effect.

Any thoughts relating to his private life were put on hold. And that included Tasha.

Tonight he would focus on all matters of a personal nature. He had the weekend, and he intended to convince Tasha to remain with him. Dammit, he'd make sure of it.

Meanwhile, the current brief and his appearance in court held prime importance.

Tasha cut the connection on her cell-phone, marked off another line on her list, and walked from her office to the reception area to greet her eleven-thirty appointment.

An hour later she made the third of six private calls, tended to some paperwork, then she took a short lunch-break and completed the remaining calls.

Tasha left the office early and reached the new

apartment minutes ahead of the removalist, who together with his assistant brought in and placed the furniture and variously marked crates.

The refrigerator hummed reassuringly at the flick of a switch, and she unpacked linen, consigned one set to the washing machine, then set to unpacking crockery, cutlery, pots and pans.

It was late when she finished, much later than she had anticipated. She was hungry, tired...but satisfied. All that remained for her to do tomorrow was transport all her clothes from Jared's apartment, then visit the supermarket.

An insistent peal penetrated, sounding loud in the silence of the room, and Tasha crossed to the table and retrieved her cell-phone from her bag.

'Where in hell are you?' Jared's voice held an icy anger she chose to ignore.

'I said not to wait dinner,' she managed equably, and sensed rather than heard his husky oath.

'Do you have any idea what the time is?'

She hadn't thought to look, and her eyes widened as she cast a glance at her watch. Eleven-fifteen.

'Sorry, I got carried away.' Wasn't that the truth!

'Where are you?'

There was no time like the present. 'Settling furniture into my apartment.'

The silence was so deafening it would have been possible to hear a pin drop.

'Would you care to run that by me again?' Jared queried in a tone that was silky smooth and dangerous.

'I don't believe you possess defective hearing.'

'Tasha,' he growled in warning.

'What part of "I'm moving out" didn't you understand?'

His silence was palpable, and she could sense the effort he made to retain control. 'Where are you?'

'I'll write down the address and give it to you tomorrow when I collect my clothes.' Cool, calm, *polite*. 'Goodnight.'

'You're not coming home?'

The decision was made, and she didn't intend to renege. 'I'll see you in the morning.' She ended the call before he had a chance to say another word.

She looked at the cell-phone as if it had suddenly become an alien object. Then slowly her gaze lifted and trailed the room. Dear heaven, what had she done?

Her stomach rumbled, a reminder she hadn't eaten since lunch, and she crossed to her briefcase, extracted a banana she'd bought earlier in the day, then she peeled and ate it.

Followed by a long glass of water, and she felt measurably better. She'd take a shower, make up the bed, then crawl into it and hopefully sleep.

The fact she did owed much to the events of the day, and she woke late, rose and dressed in the same clothes she'd worn the day before, then she took the lift down to basement-level and drove to a nearby bakery where she ordered croissants and tea.

The nerves inside her stomach moved from a slow

waltz to a heated tango as she used her key to enter Jared's apartment.

Part of her hoped he'd be out, but *hope* wasn't on her side, for he was there, waiting, looming large and faintly ominous, attired in black fitted jeans and a black polo top.

'If you don't mind, I'll go pack my clothes,' Tasha inclined politely, watching warily as if she expected him to pounce.

'And if I do mind?'

Her chin lifted fractionally, and she took a deep breath, then slowly released it. 'We already did this last night.' She moved towards the hallway, only to come to an abrupt halt as he moved to bar her way.

'You may have, but I'm far from done.'

'There's no point in repeating what has already been said,' she inclined politely, stepping around him as she moved a few paces to a storage cupboard and pulled down one suitcase and followed it with another, then she carried them down to the main bedroom.

Jared followed her and stood just inside the room, watching as she opened drawers and emptied their contents without any pretence at neatness.

He resembled a dark angel, tall, broad shoulders, lean hips, long legs, and the face of a brooding warrior. Control, he had it...but for how long?

She'd never had reason to test it before, and she wasn't sure she wanted to begin now.

'There's nothing I can do or say to change your mind?'

The words held a dangerous edge she chose to ignore. 'No.' It sounded final…too final. Pain shafted through her body, and her breath caught at its intensity.

Get a grip, she mentally chastised. You've made your decision, so just…get on with it.

She crossed to the walk-in wardrobe and began sliding clothes from hangers. Two suitcases weren't going to do it, she perceived. If she piled her work suits on the back seat of the car and stowed the suitcases in the boot she should be able to make one trip.

'You perceive our relationship as being over?'

The silkiness in his voice slithered like ice down the length of her spine, and each word pierced her emotional heart.

Tasha carried out an armful of garments and placed them carefully on the bed, then she turned to look at him…and almost wished she hadn't.

There was something evident in his features she'd never seen before. A hardness, a distancing that tore at her in a way that made her want to retract her words.

'I think we both need to take some time out,' she said carefully.

'And you moving to another apartment will work?'

She held his gaze. 'I don't know.'

'You're carrying my child.'

Dear heaven, what was she *doing*? 'Please,' she

begged, aware of the ache of unshed tears. 'Don't make this more difficult than it is.'

He could verbally tear her to shreds, and it said much he resisted the temptation to do so. 'You expect me to stand here and not fight to keep you?'

Her eyes filled, and she barely held on to her composure. 'I'm not walking out of your life.'

'Just out of my apartment.'

She wasn't able to utter a word for the lump that had risen in her throat. 'Yes,' she managed at last.

'The object of the exercise is to acquire independence and some space?' He didn't like the idea, but he could handle it.

She stood motionless for a few seconds. 'Yes.' Civility, politeness, even gratitude. She could do that. Without a further word she turned and walked back to the walk-in wardrobe to collect the remaining clothes.

When it was done, Jared collected his keys and carried the cases out to the lift.

'I can manage them.'

He swept her a brief, hard look. 'I'll follow you in my car.'

'That's not—'

'Shut up.' The command was silk-soft and deadly, and her mouth thinned as the lift doors swept open.

She didn't offer a word during the descent, nor did she comment when he slung her luggage into the boot of his car.

Instead she slid behind the wheel of her BMW and drove to street-level, then took the route to her apartment, all too aware of Jared's Jaguar following close behind.

Would he approve where she'd chosen to live? She told herself she didn't care. It was her choice, her decision, and she'd be damned if she'd seek his comment.

Which was just as well, as he refrained from offering any as he followed her in and deposited the cases in the main bedroom…easy to find, as it was the only one.

Jared emerged into the lounge. 'Thanks.' Oh, hell, this was awkward.

At that moment the doorbell pealed, and Jared opened the door.

'Hi,' a pleasant male voice greeted. 'I'm Damian, from across the hall. And you are?'

'Tasha's partner,' Jared drawled, which drew raised eyebrows in response.

'Yet she's moving in alone.'

'Not by my choice.'

Tasha drew level with the doorway and incurred a soft, appreciative whistle from a young man who resembled a graduate fresh out of university, tall, lean and…well, fresh, she perceived as she offered a musing smile. 'Tasha.'

'Ah. So I can look, but not touch?' Damian's grin was infectious. 'Pity.' He offered Tasha a devilish wink. 'Anything you need, just call.' He turned and sauntered back to his own apartment.

Jared closed the door and swung round to face her. 'Interesting character.'

'Yes, isn't he?' She moved back a step and spared him a level look. 'Thanks for your help with the luggage. I'd offer you tea or coffee, but I haven't had a chance to get to the supermarket.'

He wanted to say something, but he bit back the words. Instead, he leant forward and laid his mouth over hers in a brief, hard kiss, then he straightened. 'Any problems, call me.'

She wasn't capable of uttering a sound, and she watched as he opened the door, then closed it quietly behind him.

She was alone. That was what she wanted…wasn't it?

Oh, dammit, this wasn't the time to stand around brooding. She needed to go shopping, she needed to unpack.

Tasha spent the weekend getting everything straight.

Jared rang each evening, and they both resorted to conversation that was courteous, but brief.

There was something to be said for having her own space, Tasha reflected as she consigned fresh fruit and milk to the refrigerator. The only person she had to please was herself. No one she was obligated to phone and say she'd be late, or unable to make dinner.

Living alone was her own decision. So why the slight twist in her stomach each time she entered her empty apartment? After three days in residence, it wasn't getting any easier.

Stop it, she silently admonished. You wanted this, you've got it…so live with it.

The alternative…let's not go there.

She moved through to the bedroom, caught up fresh underwear and made for the bathroom, where she discarded her clothes, then stepped beneath the shower.

A dinner invitation, Jared had reminded when he rang, issued by the Haight-Smythes a fortnight ago and one he felt obliged to keep.

Tasha's first thought was to refuse. Any soirée hosted by Jonathon and Emily Haight-Smythe was an *occasion* attended by the cream of the city's social echelon.

It meant dressing to kill, air-kisses and indulging in scintillating conversation. None of which particularly appealed.

A challenge, she assured as she applied make-up and styled her hair. Her first choice was a black figure-hugging gown, all but strapless except for tiny lace cap sleeves. Except even with blusher and a deep rose lip-colour she looked far too pale and wan.

Red, she decided, with its bias-cut panels, clever frills and side-split.

Matching shoes and evening bag made it a heart-stopping ensemble, and she swept her hair high, added ear-studs, a pendant.

She entered the lounge as the intercom buzzed. Jared, right on time.

'I'm on my way down.'

He was waiting in the lobby, a tall, dark angel

whose height and breadth of shoulder were emphasised by an immaculate dinner suit, dark blue shirt and matching silk tie.

His facial features were achingly familiar, and all her sensory impulses came alive in primitive recognition.

How was it possible for one man to invade her senses to this degree? To be so attuned to him, mentally, emotionally, spiritually, it seemed as if her heart, her soul meshed with his to become one.

Even now, she had to physically restrain herself from seeking his embrace, linking her hands together at his nape as she pulled his head down to hers.

She wanted, needed his touch, his taste as his tongue mated with her own in a sensuous dance that was a prelude to how the evening would end.

Anticipation. The light teasing, a musing smile, a tantalising promise.

'Hi.' As a greeting it was carelessly casual, as she meant it to be.

'Tasha,' Jared acknowledged. 'How are you?' He moved forward and brushed his lips to her temple.

It wasn't enough, and it left her feeling more disturbed than she was prepared to admit.

'Fine.' And she was, physically. In fact she felt disgustingly healthy. 'Shall we leave?'

The Haight-Smythe residence nestled across the river against the curve of a hill in suburban Ascot, where stately homes merged with imposing modern structures. Old and new money meshed with graceful style, the streets rimmed by leafy trees and neat grass verges.

Emily and Jonathon's home had been built at the beginning of the twentieth century, and faithfully renovated, restored and maintained to closely resemble the original. Ornate pressed ceilings with elaborately designed cornices, highly polished parquet floors covered in part with lush oriental rugs. Expensive curtains, antique furniture, magnificent original works of art graced the walls.

Elegance personified, Tasha accorded as she accepted orange juice from a proffered tray and allowed her gaze to drift idly around the room.

Most of their fellow guests were known to her, and it was remarkably easy to mingle at Jared's side, exchange a few pleasantries, smile and converse as if everything in her world was exactly the same as it had been a week ago.

Except it wasn't, and she was supremely aware of the difference.

Body language could be more revealing than one expected, and, although she failed to detect any artificiality in Jared's attitude towards her, she felt as if her body was a tightly coiled spring.

Was her smile a little too bright? Her tone tinged with something indefinable? Did her usual warmth and spontaneity seem too contrived?

'Relax,' Jared drawled, watchful of the slightest change in her expression. Did she know he could define the direction of her thoughts?

Right now she'd prefer to be anywhere else but

here. It would have been easy for her to opt out of tonight's invitation, plead a headache or any minor ailment as a suitable excuse. Except she hadn't. Sheer stubborn-mindedness, or the challenge of playing the social game?

'What makes you think I'm not?'

He picked up her hand and lightly traced the veins inside her wrist. The pulse beat fast there, and he soothed it, stilling her effort to pull free.

'Jared.'

The well-modulated feminine voice was familiar, and Tasha turned slightly to face Soleil Emile, the daughter and third-generation Emile of the prestigious legal firm, Emile and Associates.

Tall, slender, with long, lustrous auburn hair, Soleil resembled a model playing at the legal role of solicitor. Her mode of attire was European designer label, her footwear hand-tooled from the finest shoemakers in Italy and France.

It irked that Soleil excelled at her job, and proved a minor irritation when the glamorous Soleil frequently managed to be the solicitor at Jared's side in the courtroom.

Had they enjoyed an affair? Jared, when Tasha asked, had uttered an amused denial. Soleil, however, liked to infer the friendship was something more than professional.

Why query it now? Tasha demanded silently. Because if Soleil caught so much as a whisper Jared and Tasha were no longer an item, Soleil would zoom in for the kill.

The mere thought acted like an arrow piercing her heart. 'Soleil,' she managed with admirable politeness.

It was all terribly civil, Tasha reflected as they indulged in social pleasantries. Talking 'shop' in general terms was permissible. Openly discussing a case or a client was not.

'You won't mind if I steal Jared for a short while later in the evening?' Soleil didn't wait for an answer as she turned towards Jared. 'I'll confirm the information via email, but I'd like the opportunity to put you in the picture.'

Who did she think she was kidding? The only picture Soleil was interested in had everything to do with Jared North, the man.

How could Jared be so blind to imagine Soleil had only his current legal brief in mind?

Or was he aware of Soleil's guise, and skilfully kept the relationship on a strictly professional basis?

For heaven's sake, get a grip, Tasha chided silently. Soleil has been a part of Jared's professional life for as long as you've known him. Why choose to agonise about it now?

'If you'll excuse me?'

Tasha detected the sensual purr beneath the polite veneer, and barely restrained a retaliatory feline growl as Soleil glided gracefully away.

Dinner was announced a short while later, and it proved to be a culinary triumph served with sophisticated flair.

Jared was attentive, more so than usual, and at

one stage she leaned in close, offered him a sweet smile and said quietly, 'You're verging close to overkill.'

'Think so?'

His voice was low, husky, and far too intimate for her peace of mind. Did he have any idea of the effect he had on her?

Without doubt. They shared a history together, the memory of which was hauntingly vivid. His mouth, the touch of his hands, the way he used both to drive her wild. Beyond reason, where intense passion ruled, transcending anything she'd known or imagined possible.

And you're giving this up? a tiny voice taunted mercilessly. *Are you mad?*

Was it expecting too much to want it all? Were her expectations too high, too impossible to achieve?

In all honesty she had to admit she'd considered marriage to Jared a possibility...correction, probability. She'd been reasonably positive their relationship held a relative permanency when they chose to live together.

Yet he hadn't mentioned marriage, and she mentally questioned if he observed the axiom 'if it ain't broke, don't fix it'?

'Want to share?'

Tasha returned to the present in a second, and she managed a faint smile. 'Not particularly.' At least, not now, not here.

She glimpsed something in his dark gaze, fleeting

and indefinable, then it was gone. Surprise widened her eyes as he caught her hand and lifted it to his lips, and for a few seconds she became lost in the evocative warmth his gesture generated.

How could she do that when she was at odds with him? It irked unbearably the pull of the senses was stronger than her capacity to control them...even briefly.

Was he aware of it? Deliberately instigating a public gesture as a reminder?

He lowered their hands to rest on his thigh, and his fingers tightened as she made a furtive effort to pull free.

Dessert was a delightful concoction, and Tasha used a dessert fork in one hand whilst conducting a silent battle with the other.

Did anyone notice? Somehow she doubted it, for the conversation flowed, as did the wine, and there was a sense of relief as the dessert plates were removed and guests were invited to sample a variety of cheeses from a well-stocked platter.

Eventually the meal came to a close and Emily encouraged her guests to adjourn to the lounge for coffee.

Tasha was aware of Jared's hand against the small of her back as they vacated the dining-room. 'Must you?' she demanded quietly beneath the veneer of a soft smile, and met his hooded appraisal.

She was behaving out of character, and it didn't sit well. An apology hovered on her lips, yet it remained unuttered as a fellow guest claimed his attention.

She requested tea, accepted the delicate china cup and saucer from their hostess, and moved a few paces to join Jonathan Haight-Smythe.

A supreme-court judge, he'd witnessed every aspect of human nature, mediated, adjudicated, and directed the course of justice. Inside the courtroom he was known to be a stickler for protocol, intolerant of grandstanding, and unsympathetic to anyone who attempted to pervert judicial action.

'Tasha, how nice you were able to join us tonight.'

'A lovely meal and delightful company,' she complimented with sincerity. 'Thank you for the invitation.'

'Our pleasure. One trusts the corporate world is treating you well?'

The mores and vagaries of the legal fraternity were complex, and Tasha managed a suitably innocuous response that earned a solemn smile.

Soleil, she noted idly, had managed to capture Jared's attention and the image of his head inclined towards hers remained as a photographic visualisation that continued to haunt during the evening.

Tasha was deep in conversation with the wife of a noted prosecuting attorney when she sensed Jared's presence at her side.

She possessed an internal antenna where he was concerned, almost a sixth sense that was as uncanny as it was surprising. A few weeks ago she would have viewed the feeling with benevolent affection, mentally waxing lyrical they might have known each other in another life…perhaps twin halves of a soul.

Now it was accompanied by an unaccustomed ache in the region of her heart that had little to do with anything she cared to name.

'You'll excuse us, Jonathon?'

Jared's voice was silk-smooth, polite with the merest edge. Tasha wondered at it, and the coil of tension emanating from his powerful body.

This close she could sense the faint drift of his exclusive cologne mingling with the scent of freshly laundered cotton, the elusive smell of expensive cloth used by the Italian tailor who'd fashioned his suit.

Old money, inherited through several generations, wisely invested to ensure wealth built and multiplied during the lifetimes of several highly professional men.

Jared, she knew, was pursued for his wealth and social standing. Beneath the sophisticated façade was an innate wariness, a cynicism prepared to deal with the social climbers and opportunists. An undetectable barrier only those very close to him were aware of.

It had amused him when she'd refused to accept his gifts, with the exception of birthdays and Christmas.

She could recall informing him with solemn dignity that, while she appreciated his intention, she believed the most important gift was beyond price...and he'd already gifted her that. Himself.

Now she wasn't so sure.

'You'll excuse us if we leave?' Jared inclined, reaching for her hand as he offered Jonathon a salutary compliment. 'There are a few aspects I need to clarify in my notes before tomorrow's session.'

Five minutes later Tasha buckled the seat belt as Jared slid in behind the wheel, fired the engine, then he eased the car down the driveway and onto the street.

A sudden shower swept in, lashing the windscreen with rain, only to ease to a light drizzle within minutes.

At this evening hour the traffic had slowed considerably, and Jared brought the car to a smooth halt in a parking bay adjacent to the main entrance to her apartment building, then cut the engine and doused the lights.

Tasha reached for the door clasp. 'Thanks for the ride.'

He rested a forearm on the steering wheel and leaned towards her. 'Why the hurry?'

Because if he touched her, she'd be lost. 'You expressed the need to go through your notes.'

'Concern for my welfare, Tasha?'

'Your client,' she corrected evenly, and her eyes widened as he captured her face.

'How considerate.' He lowered his head and brushed his mouth to hers in a slow, sweet kiss.

Dear heaven. It took all her strength not to respond to the light graze of his teeth, and a low groan rose and died in her throat as he took her deep in an evocative sensual onslaught that left her wanting more.

So much more, she despaired, aware just how easy it would be to succumb to his persuasive touch. There was a part of her that wanted to fist his shirt in one hand and drag him indoors, ride the lift to her apartment, and tear off his clothes as she pulled him into the bedroom.

She wanted his mouth at her breast, the feel of his arousal against her belly, his hands...and she wanted to touch him, savour the taste of his skin, absorb his male essence, in a no-holds-barred mating that took sexual hunger to a new dimension.

A faint whimper escaped from her throat as Jared eased back a little, and for a wild moment she clung to him, on the verge of beseeching him for more.

Oh, God. Words rose to the surface, and she held them back with difficulty. The blood drained from her face, leaving it pale in the reflected outdoor lighting, and her eyes were large from shock and unshed tears.

His fingers brushed her cheek, then settled at the edge of her mouth to linger and lightly trace the soft contours of her lips swollen from his kiss.

He wanted to make love with her. Hold her close, and never let her go. And he would...soon. For now, he had to give her the time and space she vowed she needed. But not for long.

'I left making out in cars behind with my teens,' he teased musingly.

She had to try for levity. Anything else would be a recipe for disaster…hers. 'Would that have been the BMW, Jag, four-wheel-drive? Or had you progressed to a Porsche?'

'I remember the occasion, but not the vehicle.' His response brought the reaction he coveted…a light-hearted laugh.

'And the girl?'

'Some were more memorable than others.' But none who came close to you, he added silently.

There was an awkward silence, one neither of them rushed to fill. Then Tasha drew apart from him and unlatched the door. 'Goodnight.'

He watched as she slid from the car. 'I'll call you.'

Jared waited as she used a coded key to open the outer door, then bypass the security system. She didn't look back as she stepped towards the bank of lifts, and he only fired the engine when the lift doors closed behind her.

CHAPTER FIVE

IN a way it was a relief to absorb the extra workload distribution incurred by an associate absent due to emergency family leave, for it kept Tasha busy with little time to think or brood on personal issues.

Or at least that was what she told herself.

In reality Jared's image was *there*, so frequently to the forefront of her mind she had to school herself to focus on the work in hand.

Mistakes were inexcusable, and she went to painstaking lengths to ensure none was made. 'Autopilot' mode wasn't an option.

Just as she thought she had a handle on things there was a call from Reception.

'There's a special delivery for you,' Amanda informed.

Tasha checked her watch and verified she had five minutes before a client appointment. 'I'll be right out.'

She was expecting a contract via courier service, a document she needed to peruse and compile an overview of before presenting it to an associate colleague the next day. Legalese presented a multifaceted minefield which could prove hazardous to the unwary. Each clause required close examination to ensure there were no loopholes and locked in a client's express needs.

Except it wasn't a slim courier package on Amanda's reception desk. Instead, a large bouquet of red roses bound in Cellophane reposed there, and her stomach lurched at the thought of who had sent them.

'Special occasion, or something?'

Tasha managed a smile. 'Or something.'

'I'll organise a vase,' Amanda declared with friendly efficiency.

'Thanks.' She caught up the bouquet and waited until she was in her office before extracting the card.

'Love, Jared'.

Love? That was a joke. Did he even comprehend the true meaning of the word?

His interpretation didn't match her own. And if he thought a bouquet of roses would soften her resolve, then he was way off base.

In the privacy of her office she took a few seconds to admire the perfect velvet-petalled buds, and she inhaled their scent, remembering other occasions when Jared had gifted her roses.

Don't go there.

There was a tap on her door, and she hurriedly composed herself as she bade entry.

'Vase with water,' Amanda said cheerfully as she deposited it on a credenza. 'Want some help? Your client is waiting in Reception.'

Tasha offered a warm smile. 'Thanks. Give me a minute, then show her in.'

The courier duly delivered the contract, which she perused over lunch sent out for and eaten at her desk. She noted down queries, points of reference, then she dealt with what the afternoon threw at her, staying back an hour before driving home.

Although *home* was a misnomer, and there was a teeth-gnashing moment when she automatically entered a familiar traffic lane on exiting her office block...only to discover at the next intersection it would lead her over the river *en route* to Jared's apartment. A muttered imprecation at her absent-mindedness was followed by something more explicit when no one would allow her to switch lanes...which meant she was trapped into following a route she didn't want.

It was several minutes before she could divert and backtrack, and she ignored the insistent peal of her cell-phone, choosing to let the call go to message-bank.

Jared. He could wait, she decided, until she'd had something to eat and taken time to relax and unwind a little from a hectic day. One that was far from done, for she needed to go through her notes, check references, and compile a suitable précis. An early night wasn't going to be an option.

First she needed to slip out of her stiletto heels and exchange her formal suit for casual attire, then she'd unpin her hair from its smooth twist and cleanse off her make-up.

A chicken salad sufficed as dinner, and she added

some fruit, then she took bottled water from the refrigerator and set up her laptop at the kitchen table.

She was on to the third reference analysis when the doorbell pealed, and she stilled momentarily, curious when the only person to her knowledge who knew her new address was Jared. Given the building's security, he'd have had to buzz her first before gaining entry.

Cautious, she checked the peephole, identified her immediate neighbour, and unlocked the door.

'Damian.' His infectious grin brought forth a faint smile. 'Is this a social call? I'm kind of busy right now.'

'Social. I'm meeting up with a few friends at a downtown café, and thought you might like to join us.'

'Thanks, but—'

'No, thanks?' he interceded with a quizzical lift of one eyebrow.

'Another time, perhaps?'

The insistent peal of her cell-phone proved an interruption, and she lifted both hands in an apologetic gesture. 'I'd better take that.'

She closed the door, then picked up on the call.

'Rough day?'

Her toes curled at the sound of Jared's deep drawl, and she closed her eyes in self-directed exasperation at the effect he had on her nervous system.

'You could say that,' she managed politely, then memory and good manners rose to the surface.

'Thanks for the roses.' She'd left them at the office. In the morning she intended to shift them out to Reception for the firm's clientele to enjoy.

'My pleasure.'

Just thinking what his *pleasure* could involve sent her pulse into overdrive. 'Is there a particular reason for your call?'

'Other than to say *hello*?'

She bit back an expressive sigh. 'I've brought work home, I have at least three hours ahead of me, and I'm—'

'Have you eaten?'

Her fingers tightened round the cell-phone. 'What is this? Check-up time?'

'A simple *yes* or *no* will suffice.'

'Yes.'

'Shall we start over?' He sounded vaguely amused.

'As in?'

'I was going to suggest we go somewhere for coffee.'

'I'm not dressed to go anywhere.'

'We don't necessarily have to go out.'

Staying in held implications she didn't care to pursue. 'I don't think that's a good idea.'

Sometimes it was necessary to lose a battle in order to win the war. 'Not if you need to work late. Goodnight, Tasha. Sleep well.'

Who did he think he was, keeping tabs on her? She felt inclined to call him back and tell him just what she thought of him!

She was about to dial his number when the cellphone rang.

She activated the call and recited her personalised series of digits, then uttered a curt, 'Yes?'

'Is this a bad time?'

'Eloise.' She took a deep breath and released it. 'Hi.'

'Lunch, tomorrow? That lovely place upstairs in the gallery of the Brisbane arcade? One o'clock?'

'Love to. Shall I ring and book a table?'

'I'll take care of it. Are you OK?'

'I'm fine,' she assured, and knew she lied. 'Just a bad day, staff away, a work overload. You know how it goes.'

'We'll talk tomorrow.'

Tasha arrived late through no fault of her own, gave her order, and prepared for a barrage of questions.

Eloise didn't disappoint, and after requesting a detailed description of the apartment, the move, work...the next subject was Jared.

'We speak on the phone,' Tasha admitted and caught a speculative gleam as Eloise queried,

'Have you been out together?'

'Not exactly.'

'Sweetheart, either you have or you haven't.'

She shrugged. 'Dinner on Monday in response to an invitation issued a couple of weeks ago.'

'And?'

'There is no *and*,' she refuted firmly.

'Like, it was a *date*? Jared picked you up and dropped you home again? No—'

'No,' Tasha interrupted firmly.

'I'm impressed.' Eloise offered an infectious smile. 'Anything else?'

'You're unconscionable.'

'I'm also your very best friend.'

A friendship that extended way back to junior-grade school. They'd shared teenage years, been there for each other during the bad times. Eloise's parents' divorce was one of them. Tasha's father's succession of failed marriages numbered five at the last count, and the last she'd heard he was courting a wealthy Texan widow. Tasha had no sooner become used to one stepmother when there was another lined up waiting to take her place.

It hadn't made for a stable upbringing, and boarding-school had become a haven, together with a resolve to get a law degree and succeed.

Tasha covered Eloise's hand with her own. 'I know.' She worried her bottom lip with the edge of her teeth. 'He sent me roses.'

'The man adores you,' Eloise said with certainty.

'He enjoyed what we had,' she amended. 'A comfortable lifestyle, commitment to each other, no strings. At least not the ties that bind.'

'And you want those ties?'

Her eyes darkened and she dug fingernails into her palm. 'For the right reasons.' She picked up her teacup and was surprised to discover her hand was trembling. 'Do you blame me? My father hasn't exactly provided a shining example of wedded bliss.'

'It doesn't mean you'll follow the same pattern,' Eloise said gently.

Tasha replaced the cup and checked her watch. 'I have to get back. You don't need to leave. Stay and finish your coffee. I'm taking care of the tab.'

'No, you're not.'

'Humour me. You can pick up on the next one.'

Tasha woke next morning at the sound of the alarm, stretched, then made a dash for the bathroom.

Dear heaven, if this was morning sickness, she didn't want it!

Hot sweet tea and toast. It had worked yesterday. It had better work today, she vowed grimly as she stepped into the kitchen. The shower could wait...everything could wait until her stomach settled.

Some pregnant women, she'd read in the pregnancy bible, suffered sickness symptoms morning, noon and night. For the entire nine months.

She placed a hand over her stomach. 'Baby,' she admonished huskily, 'if you do the morning, noon and night thing to me, Mama is going to utter words your tender ears should never hear!'

Within half an hour she felt relatively human, and she hurriedly showered, dressed, and left for the city.

As days went, hers was a doozy.

It was bad enough she was running late, a situation made worse when her car refused to start. No mechanic, she nevertheless checked the rudimentary possibilities, then switched on the ignition. Nothing.

Hell and damnation.

'Trouble?' a voice queried, and she turned, recognised Damian, and threw her hands up in the air.

'It won't start.'

He popped the hood and fiddled, then slid in behind the wheel, twisted the key in the ignition, then pursed his lips. 'Battery. Dead as a dodo.'

As she saw it, she had two choices. Organise a replacement and be late in to the office. Or call a taxi.

'Leave your car key with Management,' Damian suggested. 'I'll drop you into the city, and you can use your cell-phone to arrange with a mobile battery service to instal a replacement and bill you.'

Constructive help was a godsend, and she told him so. 'I owe you one.'

Nevertheless she was late, a fact that earned a terse reprimand from an important client who made it evident he didn't appreciate cooling his heels for any reason.

From there on in, things got worse. A meeting ran over time, the secretarial pool was diminished by two absent on sick leave, resulting in documents only ranking high on priority were prepared, and lunch was something she missed entirely.

Mid-afternoon her inter-office line buzzed, and she frowned as she reached for the phone. Her next appointment wasn't due for another half-hour.

'Delivery for you,' Amanda informed with bright efficiency.

'I'll come get it.'

A single red rose in a Cellophane cylinder reposed in Reception, and Tasha met the receptionist's dreamy smile.

'Jared North is such a romantic hunk.'

Two weeks ago she would have given a delighted laugh, agreed, and become a little misty-eyed herself. Now she simply smiled and said, 'Yes, isn't he?'

When she returned to her office she retrieved her cell-phone, checked with the management office and had it confirmed a battery had been fitted in her BMW.

It was almost six when she walked out of the office building and joined a queue waiting for a taxi.

She was tired, hungry, and felt faintly incongruous holding on to a long-stemmed rose in one hand, a bulging briefcase in the other while balancing her shoulder bag.

The sound of a car horn was just one of many, and Tasha merely cast a cursory glance at the vehicle which swooped to a halt at the kerb.

The window slid down kerb-side and the male driver leaned sideways. 'Tasha. Hop in and I'll give you a lift home.'

She took a closer look, recognised Damian, hesitated, gave the lengthy queue a glance, and slid into the front passenger seat. 'Thanks.'

'No problem.' He shifted gears and sent the car

into the stream of traffic, eased into the lane that would eventually lead to Kangaroo Point, and sent her a friendly grin as he paused at the next set of lights.

'I'm going to stop for Chinese takeaway. What say I get enough for two and we share?'

It beat having to cook. 'OK, but I'm buying.'

'Will you argue if I refuse?'

'Consider it thanks for helping out this morning.'

'Your place or mine?' Damian queried half an hour later as they emerged onto their floor from the lift.

Tasha effected a light shrug. 'Doesn't matter. Yours.' she decided.

He unlocked the door and ushered her in to what was ostensibly a typical bachelor pad, huge TV screen, expensive stereo equipment, black leather sofa and chairs.

Damian placed the take-out sack on the dining-room table, collected two cans of beer from the re-frigerator, and indicated they eat.

'Not for me. I don't drink.' A new dictum, and one that would be in force for the remainder of her pregnancy.

'Cola, soda, water?'

She settled for the latter, broke open the contain-ers, and used chopsticks with practical dexterity.

'So, why does a gorgeous young thing like you choose to live alone?'

Tasha shot him a direct look. 'Is this "getting to know you" or the third degree?'

'Both.'

'With a view to…?'

'Asking for a date.' He took time to scoop up another mouthful of noodles, and swallowed them down. 'That is, if the partner is no longer a partner.' He tried for boyish helplessness, and failed miserably. 'And you'd consider going out with me.'

It was time for total honesty. 'I'm pregnant to the partner,' she said quietly. 'Who feels obligated to offer marriage.'

His expression was a study. 'Got it.'

She doubted he had. 'I hope we can still be friends.'

'I'm good with kids. Uncle to five nephews and three nieces.' He offered a wicked grin. 'Dab hand with the diaper thing.'

'Someone I can call on in a crisis.'

The grin was still in evidence. 'Don't see any reason why we can't go to a movie some time, or share a take-out.'

He was nice. 'No reason at all.' She finished the last mouthful, and reached for the glass of water just as her cell-phone rang.

Jared. 'Can I call you back?' she began without preamble.

'Of course.'

She cut the connection and slid the unit back into her bag.

'Let me guess,' Damian interposed. 'The partner?'

'You got it in one.'

'So, should you go running back to your apartment, or can you take time for tea or coffee?'

'Tea would be lovely.'

'Not going to run to his bidding, huh?' he teased. 'I admire that in a woman.' He rose to his feet and crossed into the kitchen, where he filled and plugged in the electric kettle.

Tasha took her time drinking the tea. Damian was easy to talk to, interesting, and pleasant company.

Consequently it was almost an hour later when she bade Damian 'goodnight' and crossed the hall to let herself into her apartment.

With automatic movements she dropped her briefcase, then she undid the Cellophane cylinder and deposited the rose in water. Next she turned on the television, then crossed into the bedroom, undressed, and took a leisurely shower.

Towelled dry, she pulled on a nightshirt, added a robe, then she picked up the phone and dialled Jared's number.

'It's unnecessary for you to ring me every day,' Tasha said coolly when he picked up.

'Get used to it.' There was an edge to his voice she chose to ignore.

'You have no right—'

'Don't even go there,' he warned. 'Shall we start over, and enquire about each other's day?'

'You want to play *polite*?'

'You want to argue?'

No, dammit, she didn't. 'So—how was your day?'

'Challenging.' It had been all of that and more. 'And you?'

'You mean, apart from the flat battery, an irate client?'

'You should have called me.'

'For what, specifically?'

'The flat battery.'

'Damian came to the rescue, and drove me into the city.'

'Did he, indeed?' Jared drawled. 'Kind of him.'

'We shared a Chinese take-out.'

'Perhaps you'd care to fill me in?'

Was there an edge to his voice? She couldn't be sure. 'He happened to drive past while I was waiting for a taxi, so he offered me a lift, and we stopped by for take-out.'

'Which you ate together where?'

She wasn't sure she liked the way this was heading. 'His apartment.'

There was a moment's silence. 'Would you like to run that by me again?'

She took a deep breath, then released it. 'Not particularly.'

'You allowed a man you'd met once, briefly, drive you into the city, willingly stepped into his car again in the evening, and you spent hours in his apartment?'

'Dammit, Jared,' she vented. 'He lives across the hall from me!'

'And that makes it all right?'

'I owed him for helping out. Sharing a take-out

meal with him was no big deal. Besides,' she added, on a roll, 'you have no right to dictate what I do, where I go, or who I spend time with!'

'That's a matter of opinion.'

Her fingers tightened until her knuckles showed white. 'I'm going to end this conversation. Goodnight.' She cut the connection and switched off the phone.

Damn him. How dared he?

Yet he has a point, a small voice taunted as she lay in bed on the edge of sleep.

Another thought occurred…and the possibility he might be jealous gave her momentary satisfaction.

CHAPTER SIX

THE phone rang just after eight, and Tasha checked the ID screen, saw the caller was Jared, and almost didn't pick up.

'I really don't want to speak to you.'

'Nothing to say, Tasha?' His voice was a musing drawl, and she mentally counted to ten.

'Don't tempt me,' she said darkly, and was maddened by his husky chuckle. 'There's a reason why you rang?' The demand was cool and incredibly polite.

'Monica is flying in tomorrow for a visit.'

His widowed mother. An extremely pleasant woman for whom Tasha held an affection. 'Oh.' Had he told her they were no longer living together?

'I thought we'd take her out to dinner and perhaps book theatre tickets for Saturday evening. She leaves Sunday for a few days on the Coast before flying home.'

'And if I say *no*?'

'She'll be incredibly disappointed at not seeing you.'

It was nothing less than the truth, and she felt truly torn. 'Dinner,' she agreed, compromising.

'I'll get back to you with details.'

So much for gaining some time and space for herself, Tasha reflected as she fought city traffic half an hour later.

It had been almost a week since she'd moved out of his apartment, yet he'd phoned every day, they'd dined out together and he'd sent flowers...red roses.

Now Monica was due in town.

Next week, who or what would it be necessitating their joint presence?

As a separation, theirs was becoming a farce.

And whose fault was that?

Tasha gained the underground car park beneath her office building, rode the lift, and became caught up with the day, only to return to her apartment that evening wondering if a 'glowing pregnancy' was merely a myth. General lassitude and mild nauseousness through the day had left her feeling anything but 'glowing'.

Now all she wanted was a shower, something to eat, then she'd curl up in a chair with a good book.

She'd just settled into the chair when the phone rang, and she gave a grateful sigh on discovering it was Eloise on the line.

'Lunch, tomorrow? One o'clock? The usual place in the Brisbane arcade? I'll ring and book a table, shall I?'

'Sounds good to me.'

'How are you feeling?'

Tasha grimaced. 'You don't really want to know.'

'Like that, is it?' Eloise said cheerfully. 'Should I ask about Jared?'

'Don't.'

'Tomorrow, Tasha. Sleep well.'

That was something she had no trouble with, and she woke next morning feeling refreshed and ready to face the day. For all of five minutes, before junior began to rock and roll and she had to make a quick dash to the bathroom.

The office was harmoniously efficient with a full complement of secretarial staff. Hence a backlog of work began to show up on her desk, and she spent time checking documentation and organising appointments.

Eloise was already seated when Tasha arrived.

'Hi, have you been waiting long?' She leant forward and bestowed an affectionate hug before slipping into the seat opposite.

Eloise's smile was warm. 'I arrived early. Now, what are you going to have?'

Tasha ordered tea, then checked the menu and made her selection.

'I didn't want to give you the news over the phone,' Eloise began as soon as a waitress served their food.

'Do I get to guess, or are you going to tell me?' she teased, for her friend was brimming over with withheld excitement.

'Simon has been offered a position in New York. We talked about it, he's accepted.' She paused for breath. 'He flies out in a fortnight, and I'll follow two weeks after him.'

'That's wonderful,' Tasha said with genuine enthusiasm. 'I'll miss you dreadfully.' And knew it to be true. One had many acquaintances, but very few really good friends.

'Hey,' Eloise chided. 'We'll email each other constantly, and I've already told Simon I'm flying back for the birth of your babe.'

'You'll do that?'

'Wouldn't miss it for the world. Besides,' she chided with mock severity, 'that little person you're carrying is going to be my godchild.'

'The honour was always going to be yours.' She glimpsed Eloise's slight frown, and queried, 'What's wrong?'

'Jared has just entered the balcony with Soleil in tow.'

Tasha felt every muscle in her body tense. 'They're headed this way?'

'Looks like it.'

'Soleil is the solicitor on Jared's case.' Couldn't be a lunch break, she rationalised. Court was already back in session for the afternoon.

'Jared has just sighted us,' Eloise enlightened. 'Soleil is trying hard not to look displeased.'

'The woman is a consummate actress.'

'Should be interesting,' Eloise said quietly an instant before her mouth curved into a warm smile. 'Jared, how nice to see you.' She inclined her head towards the woman at his side. 'Soleil.'

'Tasha.' His hand curved over her shoulder as he leaned down and brushed his lips to her cheek. 'The case adjourned until tomorrow. Soleil suggested lunch on the way back to chambers.'

I just bet she did. And of all the restaurants and café's along the mall stretch, she took a punt and chose one which, if I happened to be lunching out, I'd most likely frequent.

'Why don't you join us?' Eloise suggested sweetly, blandly ignoring Tasha's dark glance.

'We wouldn't want to interrupt your girl-talk,' Soleil declared. 'Besides, Jared and I have certain aspects of the case which require discussion.'

Tasha elected to play along. 'Confidential, naturally.' She deliberately scanned the room. 'I doubt you'll find a table. Eloise and I are just about done. You can have ours.'

'There's no need to hurry off,' Jared drawled.

Was he blind to the existing undercurrents? Somehow she doubted it. However, she had no intention of watching Soleil's attempt at one-upmanship. 'I need to get back to the office.' A bald-faced fabrication, but only she knew that. 'Eloise, this is my treat.' She stood to her feet, and, loyal ally that Eloise was, she followed suit. 'Bye, Jared. Soleil.'

'Just what do you think you're doing?' Eloise demanded *sotto voce* the instant they were out of earshot.

'Removing myself from the scene before I lapsed into impoliteness.'

'Thereby allowing Soleil to score one against you.'

'Quite frankly, I don't give a damn.'

'Yes, you do.'

They entered the main thoroughfare, and Eloise gave her a quick hug. 'Thanks for lunch. It was supposed to be my turn. Ring me.'

They turned and began walking in opposite directions, and Tasha spent the afternoon concentrating on the job in hand in the hope of dispelling an image of Jared and Soleil sharing lunch.

It was, she told herself, exactly how Jared described it. Something they'd probably done several times in the past. It didn't mean a thing. Heavens, she'd lunched and dined with colleagues on a strictly business basis.

So why did Soleil bother her so much?

Because she's a merciless schemer who'll stop at nothing to get what she wants.

Someone who didn't hesitate to press any advantage home, she determined when Amanda announced Soleil Emile was on line two.

Tasha glanced at her watch as she picked up. Four o'clock. She hadn't wasted much time.

'Soleil,' she acknowledged coolly. 'What can I do for you?'

'Just a friendly warning. I intend to make my move now you and Jared are no longer a couple.'

'Really?' She tried to sound uninterested, and didn't quite make it. 'And you deduced that news—how?'

'Does the *how* matter?'

'What took you so long?'

'To make a play for Jared?' A tinkling laugh sounded down the line. 'I do possess some scruples.'

And pigs fly, Tasha accorded in silent derision. 'Am I supposed to wish you "good luck"?'

Soleil's tinkling laugh sent Tasha's blood pressure up at least ten points. 'I make it a practice never to rely on luck.'

'Is that it, Soleil? I have a client waiting.' She didn't, but Soleil wasn't to know that.

'I think so.'

Tasha ended the call, and resisted the temptation to throw something.

The aggravation remained as she battled traffic *en route* to her apartment, so much so she muttered something reprehensible when another driver cut her up.

Damian was waiting at the lift well when she parked her car, and he held the lift.

'Wow, I hope it's not me you're mad at.' He pressed the appropriate button on the instrument panel. 'The partner?' he hazarded as the lift sped rapidly upward. 'Work?'

'Take your pick.'

'Well, now, I have just the remedy.' He offered her a cheeky grin as the lift slid to a halt and they emerged into the lobby. 'Go get rid of your brief-case, change out of the corporate gear, and we'll go grab something to eat and take in a movie.'

Why not? 'You don't have anything better to do?'

'Not a thing.' He took out his keys and inserted one into the door lock. 'Ten minutes OK with you?'

They went in his car, had hamburgers and fries, then chose a comedy at the nearest cinema-plex.

The movie was a riot, and there had to be some truth in laughter being the best medicine, for she emerged feeling in a great mood.

Until she caught sight of an auburn-haired, green-eyed witch of a woman who saw her at the same moment and was bent on making her presence felt.

'Well, this is a coincidence,' Soleil all but purred as she drew level. She looked pointedly at Damian and lifted an enquiring eyebrow. 'Aren't you going to introduce me?'

Tasha opened her mouth, but Damian spoke first. 'Damian. One of Tasha's friends.'

'Really? A business acquaintance?'

'No.'

Soleil shifted her gaze to Tasha. 'I must tell Jared we met.'

'Do that, Soleil,' Tasha encouraged, and tucked her hand through Damian's arm. 'You'll excuse us?'

He caught on quick, and led the way out of the auditorium. 'I gather she's not one of your favourite people?'

'How did you guess?'

'Oh, just the fact you could cut the air with a knife, and you were on the verge of challenging pistols at dawn.' He wriggled his eyebrows with comical amusement. 'Little things like that.'

'You're good.'

'I can do better. She has her eye on the partner?'

'His name is Jared.'

'I take it she doesn't know about your pregnancy?'

'In a word—no.'

'Doesn't matter.' They reached the car, which he unlocked, and she slid into the passenger seat.

'Within a week or two Jared is going to sweep you back into his apartment, his life, and Soleil won't exist…if she ever did.'

'What planet are you from?' she teased, and he lifted his hands in the air.

'The man is no fool. He might be cutting you some slack now, but soon he's going to reel you in.'

She looked at him as he fired the ignition. 'What if I don't want to be reeled in?'

He shot her a piercing glance. 'Don't you?'

Oh, hell. She wasn't sure she was ready for such in-depth perception.

They completed the distance to Kangaroo Point in silence, and as they emerged from the lift Tasha touched a light hand to his arm.

'Thanks. It was a great evening. I'd like to do it again some time if it's OK with you.'

His smile lit up his pleasant features. 'All you need to do is say the word.' He paused, then added, 'Call if you need me.'

She entered her apartment, secured the lock, then stepped into her room, shed her clothes and slid in between the bedcovers.

Sharing dinner with Jared's mother had always been a pleasant experience, and Tasha liked to think that two years' acquaintance had promoted a warm friendship between them.

Did Monica assume Tasha's live-in relationship with Jared would eventually lead to something permanent? Such as marriage? Children? Was that something she hoped for?

Infinitely tactful, Monica had been careful not to allude to anything, and, as no engagement had been announced, the woman could be forgiven for wondering how her son regarded the relationship.

Consequently, Tasha viewed the evening with a degree of mild trepidation.

In the need to dredge up her reserves of confidence, she selected an elegant trouser suit in a brilliant red, stepped into stilettos, kept her make-up to a minimum except for matching lipstick, gloss, and paid attention to her eyes.

Jared had indicated six, and she left her apartment at five fifty-five, took the lift down to the main lobby, and emerged just as Jared's Jaguar drew to a halt at the front entrance.

For a brief moment she wondered what Jared had told his mother about his and Tasha's separate living arrangements. Would there be silent reproof or disappointment evident in Monica's greeting?

As to the pregnancy…had he mentioned anything in advance of this evening, or did he intend dropping the news like a bombshell over dinner?

How did she greet him? A simple 'hello' seemed inadequate, yet—

Jared took the decision out of her hands by lowering his head and closing his mouth over hers in a brief but evocative tongue-tangling kiss that succeeded in bringing alive each and every separate nerve-end.

It wasn't fair, *he* wasn't playing fair, and if it hadn't been for his mother's presence she would have torn strips off him.

'Tasha.' Monica stepped forward and took hold of her hands. 'It's so good to see you again.'

'Likewise,' she agreed warmly. 'I believe you're heading down to the Coast for a few days.'

They moved to the car, and Jared opened both front and rear passenger doors.

'You sit in front, my dear,' Monica indicated, and shook her head as Tasha voiced a refusal. 'I insist.'

Deliberately coupling her with Jared, she acknowledged as he eased the car out onto the road.

The restaurant he'd chosen was one of the city's finest, well known for its superb cuisine. The *maître d'* greeted Jared with great deference and led them to a coveted table.

'You must tell me all your news,' Monica invited as they waited for the wine steward to deliver their drinks.

Here was the moment she'd been unconsciously waiting for. Should she go with truth or fiction? She decided to hedge her bets. 'You mean, apart from moving into my own apartment?'

'I'm sure you had a very good reason.'

Tasha met Jared's inscrutable gaze, and was unable to discern anything from his expression.

The arrival of the wine steward brought the conversation to a halt, and Jared waited until the waiter was out of earshot.

'The floor is all yours.' His indolent drawl held a tinge of silk, and she threw him a killing glare.

'You're so good with words.' Let him take the hot seat! 'I think you should tell Monica.'

His soft laughter almost undid her. 'I assure you she'll be delighted to hear she's going to be a grandmother.'

'You're having a baby?' Surprised joy lit her attractive features. 'Oh, I'm so happy for you both.' She pressed her hands together and leaned forward. 'My dear, are you keeping well?'

'The mornings aren't so good,' Jared drawled. 'And yes,' he added to what he anticipated would be Monica's next question, 'I've asked Tasha to marry me.'

'My dear, if I can help with wedding plans, please let me know.'

And now came the difficult part. 'There isn't going to be a wedding,' she said gently. 'The pregnancy was unplanned.'

Monica turned towards her son. 'Jared?'

'I'm working on it,' he assured.

Was he, indeed?

It was as well the waiter presented their starters, and Tasha had to admire Monica for keeping the conversational ball rolling.

Jared's mother was active with various charity committees, and led a busy social existence. She had many amusing anecdotes to relay, and Tasha began to relax a little.

'There was a terribly embarrassing moment at the close of the summer-collection showing last month when one of the models refused to part with jewellery lent for the occasion. It took some diplomatic soothing of ruffled feathers, a quiet but official word from the head of security before she graciously conceded to a misunderstanding.'

'Tricky,' Tasha ventured, and Monica chuckled at the memory.

'Very.' She shook her head as Jared indicated if she wanted more wine. 'I'm really looking forward to the theatre production. I have great respect for David Williamson's work.'

The food was divine, and Tasha spared an envious glance at Jared's plate. He'd ordered a prawn dish and they looked plump and succulent.

He cast her a warm smile and speared one with his fork. 'Try this.' He lifted it to her mouth, and she bit into the delicate white flesh, tasted the sauce accompanying it, and almost sighed with enjoyment.

He speared another and fed it to her, and she was supremely conscious of the intimacy of the gesture. She became caught up in the spell of it, the primitive alchemy that existed between them, and for a moment she wished she could turn back the clock to a time when everything was right between them.

Could it be again?

Possibly, she qualified. Except the doubt would always be there. She didn't want a marriage built on a shaky foundation. Nor could she bear entering a marriage based on the premise that if it didn't work out, divorce was an easy answer. As her father had. Without thought to how the consequences of his actions might affect the children of those subsequent marriages. Did he know what it was like to hold back from getting too close to any one of four stepmothers because they never stayed around very long? Or not to become fond of any young stepsiblings, because their mothers took them away?

She'd become isolated and self-sufficient, aware survival of self was of prime importance.

'Where did you go?' Jared queried quietly, observing her fleeting expression, the shadows. He wanted to gather her in, override her fears, and keep her close. So close, she'd never have reason to doubt anything again.

Tasha summoned a faint smile. 'Nowhere special.' She no longer felt hungry, and she replaced her cutlery and pushed her plate forward. 'I'm sorry.'

'No need to apologise, my dear,' Monica said gently.

Tasha declined dessert and opted for tea.

It was after ten when Jared settled the bill, and as they walked from the restaurant he caught hold of her hand and linked his fingers through her own.

His touch was warm and strong, and she didn't pull away until they reached the car.

The theatre lobby was filled with mingling patrons attired in glamorous evening attire.

Tasha recognised a few acquaintances, two clients, and offered a smile in acknowledgement as she stood with Jared and Monica.

Conversation was difficult, given the noise of muted social chatter vying with piped music.

Jared stood at her side, much too close for her peace of mind, for she could sense the strength emanating from his powerful frame, aware to a startling degree of the shape and size of him beneath the trappings of fine clothes.

She had the strangest urge to lean in against his side, have his arm circle her waist, and feel the brush of his lips against her hair.

All she had to do was shift her stance a little. Just a fraction, and the curve of her shoulder would nudge against his chest.

Think, she cautioned silently, of the consequences of such an action. She didn't play games, and pretending someone had jostled her simply wouldn't wash.

An electronic buzzer sounded, and she heard Monica's voiced relief.

'It'll be nice to take our seats. It's become a little crowded here, hasn't it?'

Tasha murmured an appropriate response as Jared moved between them as the patrons began to move towards the main entrance.

The play was a modern parody with flashes of insight and humour, the acting superb, making it an extremely pleasurable few hours that captured and entranced the audience.

Monica rhapsodised eloquently as they emerged into the foyer following the final act, and Jared chuckled a little as he brought her hand to his lips.

'I'm glad you enjoyed it.'

Tasha felt his arm along the back of her waist, the splay of his hand over her hip bone, and wondered if he knew the effect he had on her equilibrium.

A month ago she would have lifted her face and met his dark gaze with the veiled promise of how the evening would end. Smiled, even teased him a little. And relished in the anticipation, the slow building of heat until they both burned with it.

Abstinence was a bad bedfellow, and she longed for his touch, the feel of his skin beneath her lips, the silkiness as it stretched over taut muscle and sinew. His scent was an erotic aphrodisiac, one she wanted to feast with ravishing hunger.

He had the skill to turn her into a weak-willed wanton, savouring every pleasure he chose to bestow, then return it tenfold until the breath hissed between his teeth as he sought control...and lost it, taking her with him as they scaled the heights.

'Jared.'

Tasha turned slightly at the sound of that familiar feminine purr, and felt her edge of her teeth dig into the soft underside of her lip.

Soleil. Partnered by a legal associate whose name she failed to recollect.

'Amazing first night,' Soleil enthused as she

trailed perfectly manicured nails down the sleeve of Jared's jacket.

Her gaze shifted to Tasha, who gained a perfunctory acknowledgement, before taking in the older woman at Jared's side.

'Monica.'

It was a definite gush, Tasha conceded. Not overdone, but lacking in sincerity.

'How wonderful to see you again. I take it you're enjoying your visit?'

'Very much so.'

'Robert and I are going to Michael's for coffee. We'd be delighted to have you join us. It would give me the opportunity to catch up with Monica. We have a common interest in charity fundraisers.'

Oh, my. Was Jared going to buy that? The only person Soleil wanted to catch up with was *him*...and she was prepared to stretch the bounds of their professional relationship to achieve it. Her interest in charity fundraisers only extended to attending society functions in the latest designer gear and ensuring her photo with appropriate caption appeared in the glossy magazines, whereas Monica was actively involved behind the scenes, tirelessly giving her time within the various organisations.

'Thank you,' Jared inclined. 'We've made other arrangements.'

They had?

Soleil masked her disappointment with a smile that didn't reach her eyes. 'Another time, perhaps?'

'Perhaps.'

They moved with the crowd, then separated as they reached the pavement, and Monica turned towards her son.

'Thank you.'

Humour lifted the edge of his mouth. 'For what, specifically?'

'Dinner, the theatre, and excusing me from enduring Soleil Emile's company.'

'Think nothing of it.'

'I knew her mother. Nice woman. Pity her daughter didn't inherit her mother's demeanour.'

'She's very good at her job.'

His mother sent him a searching look. 'She must be, if you concede to liaise with her professionally.'

They walked the short distance to where Jared had parked the car, said their goodbyes and, although the drive to Tasha's apartment building wasn't a silent one, afterwards she had little recollection of their conversation.

'There's no need to get out,' she said quietly as Jared brought the car to a halt outside the main entrance. Except he did, anyway, walking her to the outer door and waiting as she inserted her security key.

She opened her mouth to thank him, only to have his finger press her lips closed.

'Shut up.'

It was a husky admonition as he drew her close and closed his mouth over hers with a thoroughness that staked a claim.

'I'll call you tomorrow.'

She wasn't capable of saying a word, and she stepped into the outer foyer, keyed in her code, then walked through to the bank of lifts.

The doors of one slid open immediately, and she pressed the button for her floor, then glanced towards the entrance as the doors slid closed.

Jared had moved to the car, waiting until she was out of sight.

Tasha rose early Sunday morning, and after breakfast she tidied the apartment, then, dressed casually in jeans and a loose cotton-knit top, she collected her sunglasses, keys, and rode the lift down to the basement car park.

The day beckoned, the sun shone, and the late-spring weather was warm and balmy as she drove through the city to Southbank.

She wanted to explore the markets, visit the various attractions, eat lunch at one of the outdoor cafés, and afterwards she'd stop by one of two city department stores. There were a few things she needed, and she intended to browse without the constraints of a minimum business lunch hour.

The sun was setting in a glorious blaze of orange and rose streaks in a paling sky when she drove beneath her apartment building. Her purchases reposed on the back seat, and there was a bag of Chinese take-out breathing a redolent aroma on the seat beside her.

Tasha planned nothing more vigorous than sinking into a chair, watching television as she ate, then she intended to shower and slip into bed with a good book.

The phone rang at eight, only seconds after she'd emerged from the shower, and she hurriedly grabbed a towel, then raced into the bedroom to pick up the extension.

'Tasha.'

The sound of Jared's voice sent goose-bumps scudding over the surface of her skin, and she tightened the towel she'd wound round her slender form. A gesture of self-defence?

'Jared,' she responded politely, and heard his husky chuckle. 'How are you?'

'Buried beneath a pile of law books, referencing information into the laptop. And you?'

'About to hit the bed with a good book.'

'I could offer something much more interesting.'

Her pulse quickened and began to race. 'I'm sure you could.' Just the thought of how *interesting* had heat pooling deep within. 'But you won't.' She composed herself, and kept her voice level. 'I presume there's a reason for your call?'

'I have tickets to a fundraiser at the Hilton Hotel on Tuesday evening. Valuable estate items have been donated to charity, and the executors have collaborated to hold an auction.'

Playing dress-up and indulging in the social niceties for several hours—

'It's a worthy charity.' He named it, adding, 'The catalogue lists genuine art, porcelain and jewellery.'

The 'porcelain' clinched it, as he knew it would.

'I assume you're inviting me to attend?'

He wanted to kiss and shake her, not necessarily in that order. 'Your assumption is correct.'

'In that case, yes.'

'Be ready at six-thirty. The invitation states seven, for champagne and canapés prior to the auction scheduled for eight.'

'Yessir.'

There was a measurable pause. '*Sassy* is safe over the phone, darling. Will you be so brave in person?' It was the voice he used in the night…gentle, velvet-soft, with a silky hint of promised retribution.

'You know better.' She told herself there was no quaver evident in her tone, but she had a terrible feeling she was fooling herself.

'Tuesday, Tasha. Goodnight.'

CHAPTER SEVEN

MONDAY brought the delivery of a single red rose in Reception for her, and was followed by another on Tuesday.

Tasha added each one to the vase where the others reposed, aware someone, presumably the night-time cleaners, religiously changed the water and tended to the stems, discarding a bloom only when its petals began to fall.

Choosing what to wear to the charity auction took some deliberation, and she eventually settled for a long black fitted skirt with a conventional split, a black top with silver thread, and she draped a long silk evening scarf in varying shades of silver, grey and black round her neck. Stiletto-heeled pumps completed the outfit, and she took care with her make-up, sweeping the length of her hair into a careless knot atop her head.

Jared buzzed her apartment on time, and she picked up the in-house phone. 'I'm on my way down.'

There was no doubt he looked sensational in an evening suit, white pin-tucked shirt and black bow-tie. Definitely *wow* territory, she conceded as she moved forward to greet him.

The warm gleam in those dark eyes gave her a pleasurable kick.

'If I say you look beautiful, will you hold it against me?'

'Why would I do that?'

Jared seated her in the car, then crossed round to slide in behind the wheel.

Valet parking at the Hilton made for a timely arrival, and they stepped into the main lobby, then rode the lift to the ballroom, where guests gathered in the foyer sipping champagne.

An eclectic group, Tasha noted as Jared ordered orange juice and took champagne from a proffered tray.

At seven-thirty the ballroom doors opened to allow the guests an opportunity to view the various items on display.

Security was tight, and Jared remained at her side as she headed towards the porcelain exhibits. Exquisite, delicately hand-painted pieces, some she recognised, with others she referred to the catalogue. There were crystal pieces, Baccarat and Lalique, figurines.

'See anything you particularly like?'

'It might be easier to state the ones that don't appeal.' Tasha turned towards him. 'Is there anything you'd like to view?'

Art was his preference, and it came as no surprise that he'd marked the catalogue in advance.

The Haight-Smythes were fellow guests, and they paused to exchange a few pleasantries before mov-

ing on. There would be time at the auction's conclusion to mix and mingle.

'Jared, I thought you'd attend tonight's soirée.'

Tasha turned slowly, met Soleil's deliberately
musing gaze, recognised Soleil's father, and forced
a polite greeting. She even managed what she hoped
was a warm smile.

'We'll catch you later. Father wants to examine
the jewellery.'

Had Jared known Soleil would be here tonight?

'No,' Jared said quietly, reading her mind.

Running into Soleil on every social occasion was
becoming tiresome.

'I agree.'

'You possess telepathic capabilities?'

His smile reached down and plucked her heart-
strings. 'You're an easy read.'

'Oh, great.'

'It has certain advantages.'

'Such as?'

He ran a finger lightly over her lower lip. 'It's
kept me sane.'

'I see.'

'I'm not sure you do.'

It was as well the charity chairman took the po-
dium and gave an inspiring speech before introduc-
ing the auctioneer, who announced the basic rules
of auction, indicated the first item, then declared the
bidding would begin.

It was an intriguing few hours, with a minimum

number of items passed in for failing to meet the set reserve, and the money raised by evening's end surpassed even the charity chairman's wildest expectations.

Tasha hadn't bid, but Jared did, securing a magnificent oil painting, an exquisite Lladro porcelain, and a Lalique crystal sculpture.

When financial details had been settled, guests were invited into the foyer, where champagne was offered, together with canapés, petit fours, together with coffee and tea.

It was there Soleil and her father sought Jared out, and Soleil was so incredibly *sweet* it almost made Tasha sick.

Was she trying to impress Jared or her father…or both? Whatever, she was a consummate actress. So much so, Tasha found it almost impossible not to respond in kind.

'It would appear we share a similar taste in social activities,' Tasha noted, and saw Soleil's eyes narrow.

'Brisbane's social élite frequently attend the same functions.' A light, amused laugh escaped her perfectly painted mouth. 'Let's face it, this is hardly New York.'

'I have a feeling that, even if it were, you'd still manage to hunt down your prey.'

'Oh, nasty, darling. But I'm glad you recognise my intention.' She took a moment to examine her nails before fixing Tasha with a veiled look. 'It makes it so much easier.'

'Do you think so?'

'Definitely.'

At that moment Jared took hold of her hand and lifted it to his lips. 'Ready, darling?'

'Definitely,' Tasha copied, and inclined her head towards Soleil, then her father. 'Goodnight.' She almost added 'It's been a pleasure', but decided against it. Fabrication wasn't her forte.

'Would you care to explain what that was all about?' Jared queried as they threaded their way towards the lift.

'Not really.'

'Soleil is—'

'Very good at her job,' Tasha finished as they stepped into the lift.

'Over-zealous when it comes to pursuit of men.' He punched the button that would take them down to the lobby.

'Ah, you noticed.'

They reached their destination, and Jared strolled towards the concierge, who promptly arranged for his car to be brought up from parking.

'It's an integral part of my nature.'

The Jaguar slid into sight, and the porter opened the passenger door, saw her seated, then discreetly accepted his tip.

'I'm impressed,' Tasha declared, and caught the faint cynical twist to his answering smile.

'A compliment, Tasha?' He ignited the engine.

'Perhaps,' she conceded as he eased the car forward, gained the side-road, and began negotiating inner-city one-way traffic.

It didn't take long to reach her apartment building, and she released the seat-belt and reached for the door-clasp as soon as he drew the car to a halt outside the main entrance.

'It was an interesting evening. Thank you,' Tasha added, wanting to escape, yet conversely wanting to stay.

There was a part of her that craved his mouth on hers, the intimacy of sensual contact. Except it wouldn't be enough. She'd want more, much more, and therein lay the danger.

It would be so easy to invite him into her apartment. But if she did it could only have one ending, and, while the sex would be incredible, it wouldn't solve or resolve anything.

'Goodnight.' Oh, lord, she had to get out of here before she said or did something foolish.

'You forgot something,' Jared said quietly.

He caught her startled gaze an instant before he captured her face between his hands, and kissed her. Thoroughly, with such shameless eroticism it became a total ravishment of the senses.

When he lifted his head she wasn't capable of uttering a word, and he brushed his lips to hers in a gentle gesture.

'If you don't want me to share your bed tonight, I suggest you get out of the car now.'

His husky warning was all she needed, and she slid quickly from her seat, then stepped towards the entrance, decoded the inner door, and walked through to the banks of lifts without a backwards glance.

Jared drummed fingers against his desk and admitted he'd never felt so helpless in his life. Or afraid.

In a matter of days his personal world had turned upside-down. Moved from emotional contentment and satisfaction to a place he neither liked nor coveted.

The apartment seemed empty and horribly silent. There was no light, laughing voice to greet him, no eager arms reaching for him in the night. Dear heaven, no joy without the warmth of her sweet body curled close against his own.

His control was such he could focus in the courtroom. Out of it, he merely went through the motions. Work, he buried himself in it, putting in long hours in his chambers, taking work home to labour over late into the night.

There was a part of him that found it difficult to accept Tasha's actions. *Two years*...and now suddenly it appeared as if those two years had evaporated in a puff of smoke.

Or had they?

Dammit, he'd asked her to marry him. Wasn't that enough?

Apparently not.

At first, he'd been angry. Sure in his mind she wouldn't go through with her plan to move out, and when she had, he'd been convinced it would last only a few days...a week at most.

She took his calls, answered his messages, and was so exceedingly polite it took strength of will not to shake her.

He wanted her back…in his arms, his apartment, his life. Dammit, he *needed* her.

Jared tugged fingers through his hair, ruffling its customary groomed look. He sank back in his chair and cast the neat pile of files on his desk a cursory glance, then he turned towards the plate-glass window and gazed contemplatively beyond the cityscape.

For days and far into the night he'd considered his options, presenting arguments for and against with each and every one, and had reluctantly come to the conclusion he was powerless to implement any of them.

He did, however, have an advantage in Tasha's acquiescence to continue their social obligations together.

He picked up a pen and tapped it idly against the leather-bound blotter on his desk.

She didn't seem averse to going out with him. He picked her up and dropped her back to her apartment. And she didn't ask him in.

His gaze narrowed and a soft oath escaped his throat.

They'd regressed from live-in lovers to dating. It was ridiculous.

Yet with all his legal expertise, his ability to tie his opponents into verbal knots, he had little or no power with Tasha.

Except one. Call it chemistry, sexual compatibility, shared sensuality, passion...hell, call it *love*. Whatever, the mesmeric primeval emotion existent between them was an ecstasy he'd never experienced in this lifetime. And knew deep in his gut he never would with anyone else.

Was it the same for Tasha? The answer was an unequivocal *yes*. No woman was capable of losing control to the extent she did, or becoming so wild, so totally abandoned... There were times when he'd driven her so far, so high, she'd become incandescent in his arms. *His*, only his.

Yet it was more than sex. Much more. She was his light, his heart, the very air he breathed. His reason for being.

He was damned if he'd lose her. Reduced to being a father by remote control, allowed visiting rights...and seeing another man take his place in her bed.

His hand clenched at the mere thought, and he barely controlled an animalistic snarl as the phone buzzed on his desk.

'There's a delivery for you in Reception.'

Tasha put a marker on the file she was accessing. 'I'll be right out.'

It was a boxed *something*, she saw at once, and she met Amanda's interested expression as she signed for it. 'Thanks.'

'You do intend opening it before you take it home?'

'I'll buzz you when I do.'

'Ah, hoped you might.'

'You can bring the McCormick file in at the same time.'

'Shall do.' One of the many incoming lines beeped, requiring Amanda's attention, and Tasha returned to her office.

There was a card tucked into the wrapping, and she plucked it out, opened and read the words, 'Thought this would suit your office. Jared.'

He hadn't, had he? Her fingers removed the Sellotape, the wrapping, polystyrene chips providing protective packaging for the exquisite Lladro figurine Jared had successfully bid for at auction on Tuesday night.

She touched it reverently, admiring the perfection, and carefully placed it on the mahogany credenza.

Tasha reached for her cell-phone, keyed in a text message, and sent it to him.

There was a tap on her door, and Amanda entered with the requested file.

'What do you think?' She indicated the figurine, and glimpsed the receptionist's admiration.

'It's gorgeous. Jared, of course.' Amanda placed the file down on the desk, then indicated the box and wrapping. 'Want me to take these for you?'

'Thanks.'

Tasha rang him soon after reaching her apartment, and he picked up on the fifth ring.

'Thank you,' she said with genuine sincerity. 'It's beautiful.'

'My pleasure. I enjoy gifting you things.'

A *double entendre*, if ever there was one. Tasha controlled the quivery sensation invading her body at the husky, almost sensuous tone in his voice.

'I intended calling you tonight,' Jared continued. 'You haven't forgotten we have tickets for the show at Conrad-Jupiter's Casino?'

Tasha closed her eyes, then opened them again. It had temporarily slipped her mind. Excusable, given events of the past week.

Dammit, she really wanted to see the spectacular extravaganza, had been excited when it was first advertised, delighted when Jared suggested they combine the show with a weekend at the Gold Coast. He owned an apartment in an exclusive block with beach access at Main Beach, and she adored the time they spent there.

She should refuse. 'I'd prefer not to stay over.' It was capitulation with conditions, and didn't fool him in the slightest.

'The apartment has two bedrooms.'

And that was meant to be reassurance? 'Jared—'

'Be ready at midday, Tasha.'

He ended the call before she had a chance to voice a qualifying refusal.

CHAPTER EIGHT

IT WAS insane to consider spending a weekend on the Coast with Jared. So why was she seated in the passenger seat of his car listening idly to music emitting from his CD player while attempting to focus on the passing scenery as they travelled the M1?

No matter how she justified wanting to see the live show featured at the Coast's casino, nothing changed the fact she was dicing with danger in agreeing to share his apartment overnight.

More than once she'd picked up her cell-phone to ring and cancel, only to put it off until later. Except *later* somehow never eventuated, as every time she started to dial his number she became angry with herself for wimping out.

She needed to prove she could resist him on every level, except that of *friend*. They had a future together by virtue of the child she was carrying. A friendship based on affection was better than one with acrimonious undertones.

She could play friend, and she *would*, even if it nearly killed her!

'It's a beautiful day.' Had she actually spoken those words? They sounded so banal, so…dammit, like excruciatingly polite conversation. Crazy, when she'd shared every intimacy imaginable with this man.

Just thinking about *intimacy* brought forth visions she didn't want to consider right now. Or any other time, she assured silently. That part of their relationship was over.

She adored the Gold Coast, with its shopping complexes, theme parks, waterways. All the advantages of a city without the many disadvantages. Essentially a tourist Mecca, it had a holiday atmosphere all year round.

That first glimpse of the tall high-rise buildings dotting the curved foreshore and the sparkling blue waters of the broadwater held a magic all its own.

Jared took the Main Beach turn-off and minutes later eased the Jaguar down into an underground carpark.

'We'll offload our overnight bags, then wander through to Tedder Avenue for lunch.'

'Sounds good to me,' she offered lightly as they made their way to the lift.

Tedder Avenue was a trendy area where several of the social élite chose to catch up with friends over a meal or any one of several types of coffee. For some it was brunch at Bahia, a series of lattes at Mustang Sally, then home to spend a few hours getting ready to hit one of the top restaurants in town.

Not a life Tasha would willingly choose on a permanent basis, but to indulge over a weekend offered light-hearted enjoyment.

Jared's apartment had a wealth of floor-to-ceiling

glass, open-plan living with luxurious furnishings and fittings in muted colours.

A great place to relax and unwind, Tasha accorded as she took her overnight bag into the spare bedroom and quickly extracted the outfit she intended to wear that evening and placed it on a hanger, then she caught up her shoulder bag and went out to the lounge.

Jared was standing observing the view, and he turned as she entered the room.

She was unprepared for the curling sensation deep inside, or the way her pulse seemed to pick up and race to a thudding beat.

He had it all, she perceived. The height and physique most men would envy. Sculptured bone structure and facial features made for a rugged attractiveness. Add innate sensuality, and it became one hell of a package.

Yet there was a depth to him, a development of character that included intelligence and sophisticated charm. Existent also was something indefinable, hidden deep beneath the surface. A ruthless, primitive element that boded ill for any adversary, almost lethal. A man you'd covet as friend and ally, and run far and fast if he ever became an enemy.

'Ready?'

'Yes. Let's go find some food.' The need to eat little and often had manifested itself over the past week, and although there were no visible physical changes to her body as yet, there were a few differences she'd begun to notice.

A five-minute walk brought them into the heart of Tedder Avenue, where they selected a café, chose a table and perused the menu.

'Is there anything you'd particularly like to do this afternoon?' Jared queried when they'd given their order.

A host of choices presented itself, yet she veered towards the simplistic. 'A walk along the beach, a swim.'

'No trawling the boutiques?' Jared drawled.

'There's nothing I need.' With one exception, and it couldn't be bought.

It was after three when they finished their meal, and they wandered towards the beach, then followed the sandy foreshore towards the Sheraton Mirage Hotel, where they entered the lounge bar and had a cool drink before taking the footbridge across the road to the adjacent shopping complex.

Around five they strolled back to the apartment, showered and changed ready to dine and take in the show.

Tasha had chosen to wear a black, figure-hugging dress that owed everything to its cut and design. Diamond ear-studs, a diamond pendant on a slender gold chain comprised her only jewellery, and she took care with her make-up, swept her hair into a carefree knot, teased a few tendrils free to curl at her ears, then she slid her feet into stiletto pumps and caught up an evening purse.

Jared surprised her by heading towards the Spit,

and eased the car into the entrance of the Palazzo Versace Hotel.

Upmarket, six-star and exclusive.

The concierge came forward, offered valet parking, and swiftly opened the passenger door.

Jared cast her a level glance as they entered the luxurious foyer. 'This numbers high among your favourite places.'

'Yes, it does.' She remembered the first time he'd brought her here soon after the Palazzo's official opening. Her appreciative enthusiasm for the elegant interior with its marble floors and pillars, the internal beach-pool, exquisite lighting, and the view across the broadwater encompassing the sweep of high-rise apartment buildings lining the curved foreshore.

'Thank you,' she said quietly.

'My pleasure.'

She smiled in response, chilling out from placing too much meaning on those two words, for they held connotations she didn't want to explore.

Just go with the flow, she bade silently as the *maître 'd* seated them.

Dusk was settling in, and soon darkness would fall, giving the night-scape a different dimension.

The service was excellent, the food superb, and they lingered as long as they dared before leaving for the Casino, sited a few kilometres south.

Throughout the day Tasha had become increasingly conscious of the man at her side. The light touch of his hand at the back of her waist, briefly resting on her shoulder, as he threaded his fingers through her own.

It was impossible to ignore the warmth in his gaze, or the way he affected her.

Was he aware of her increased heart-beat? The way all of her nerve-ends curled at his slightest touch?

She'd have given anything to lean in against him and lift her face for his kiss…and almost did on one occasion as a sort of reflex action so familiar it became an unconscious movement she only just checked at the last second.

The Casino was a hive of activity with people mingling everywhere, and Jared caught hold of her hand as they made their way down to the auditorium.

Spectacular, incredible…were only two of the accolades Tasha summoned to describe the live show, for the music, costumes, theme were magnificent, and she said as much during the interval.

Jared wondered if she knew how beautiful she was, not only visually, but on the inside, where it mattered. There was no artifice, no game-playing. She'd entered his life like a breath of fresh air, and had stayed.

Somehow he'd not given much thought to if or when she might leave, and if it had crossed his mind he imagined it would be *he* who did the leaving. Not the other way round.

'I wouldn't have missed this for the world,' Tasha

declared, meeting his dark, gleaming gaze. 'Isn't it fantastic?'

'Indeed. Shall we go get something to drink?'

'OK.'

They gained the foyer, and she slipped off to the powder-room while Jared fronted the bar.

When she returned he was deep in conversation with Soleil. Coincidence, Tasha wondered, or design? It seemed a little too convenient for Soleil to have booked tickets for a live show at the Coast on the same night.

A part of her registered they presented an attractive couple. Soleil's rich auburn hair was a stunning attribute. Add a faultless figure, expensive clothes, perfect facial features, and it all added up to *gorgeous*.

Jared slid an arm around her waist as she reached his side, and his smile was something else.

'Soleil.' The acknowledgement held polite warmth, a quality that was somewhat lacking in the solicitor's response.

At that moment the buzzer sounded, indicating patrons should return to the auditorium.

'Shall we say upstairs in the Atrium bar after the show?'

'Tasha?'

The last thing she wanted to do was spend social time with Soleil. Yet she fixed Jared with a brilliant smile. 'Why not?'

The remaining half of the show was equally breathtaking, the finale amazing, and there was a sense of disappointment as the curtain came down for the last time.

She was tempted to make the excuse she was tired, or nursing a headache…anything to give meeting Soleil a miss.

It would be easy enough to do, except she was loath to provide Soleil with a victory, no matter how minor it might be.

How hard had Soleil lobbied to act as Jared's solicitor? The fact she'd used unfair influence to persuade her father's recommendation was a given.

Soleil was waiting for them, and she was alone. Jared found a table, and placed an order with the waitress, then he settled well back in his chair and steered the conversation to the show.

'If you'll excuse me for a few minutes?' Tasha offered a polite smile and rose to her feet. Another change she'd discovered over the past week was the frequent need to visit a powder-room.

'I'll come with you.'

Oh, *great*. If Soleil had a girlie *tête-à-tête* in mind, she could go jump in the lake.

If Soleil made use of the facilities, she did so in record time, for she was refreshing her make-up when Tasha emerged.

'Is there any substance to the rumour you've moved out of Jared's apartment?'

Oh, my, she didn't bandy words, just aimed straight for the jugular. 'Does it look as if Jared and I are estranged?'

Soleil's mouth tightened, and her eyes took on a

hardness that was vaguely chilling. 'Answer the question, darling.'

'I'm not on a witness stand, nor am I obliged to discuss my personal life.'

'If it weren't true, you'd have issued a vehement denial.' The other woman's vividly painted mouth curved into a satisfied smile. 'Just a little warning…Jared's mine.'

'Good luck.'

'I never rely on luck.'

Tasha closed her evening purse and walked towards the door, where she turned and offered a parting shot. 'Merely manipulative engineering.'

There was something exhilarating about having the last word, although she had a dire feeling it wouldn't last long.

She arrived back at their table ahead of Soleil, and met Jared's speculative gaze with a brilliant smile.

'Should I ask?' His husky drawl held a tinge of humour.

'Don't,' she advised a few seconds ahead of Soleil's reappearance.

'Are you driving back to Brisbane tonight?' she queried as Soleil sipped her coffee.

'No. I've booked a suite at Royal Pines. I thought I might have an early round of golf.' She paused, then said smoothly as if the idea had just occurred, 'Perhaps you'd care to join me?'

To his credit Jared took his time and infused just the right degree of regret in his tone. 'Thanks for the invitation, but Tasha and I have already made plans for the day.'

None that she was aware of. 'We have?'

He offered a lazy smile. 'Yes.'

She glanced at Soleil and effected a light shrug. 'It doesn't appear golf is on his agenda.'

He drained his coffee, then fixed the bill. 'If you're ready?'

Tasha caught up her evening purse and stood to her feet. 'Enjoy your weekend, Soleil. I'm sure we'll catch up again soon.' Unfortunately.

She didn't utter so much as a word as they took the lift down to the level where Jared had parked the car.

'Would you care to tell me what that was all about?'

Tasha didn't shift her gaze, and instead she watched the tall, brightly lit apartment buildings lining the highway as they travelled the few kilometres to Main Beach.

'Soleil chose to warn me if the rumour I've moved out of your apartment is true, she intends moving in for the kill,' she relayed without preamble.

'And your response was?'

'I wished her "good luck".'

They reached the Main Beach turn-off, and within minutes Jared eased the car down into the underground car park of his apartment building.

They rode the lift and exited at their designated floor. 'Soleil bothers you?' Jared unlocked the apartment door, then tossed the keys down onto a side-table.

'She has a *thing* for you.' She moved into the lounge, stepped out of stiletto-heeled pumps, and removed her ear-studs.

'Should I be flattered?'

'Oh, for heaven's sake,' Tasha said with exasperation. 'All women between sixteen and sixty have a thing for you!' She resisted the temptation to throw something at him. 'You'd have to be blind Freddy not to notice.'

He was the antithesis of *blind*. Observing and interpreting body language was an integral part of his job. So, too, was the analysis of the human psyche.

She was all too aware he could read her like a book, and she wasn't particularly inclined to bandy words with him tonight.

She gathered up her shoes and her evening purse. 'Thanks for dinner and the show. I enjoyed both.'

'Soleil being the exception.'

Honesty forbade anything but the truth. 'Yes.' She turned and walked the few steps to the spare bedroom, entered it and quietly closed the door.

Within minutes she shed her clothes, cleansed her face of make-up, tugged on a cotton nightshirt, then she slid into bed, determinedly discarding any thought of Jared's glamorous solicitor.

She must have slept, for she woke in the dark, disoriented for a few seconds, until the need for a drink had her padding out to the kitchen.

Moonlight filtered in through the glass doors of

the lounge, and she extracted a glass, filled it with filtered water, then drank it down.

For some unknown reason she felt too restless to return to bed just yet, and she crossed through the dining area to stand gazing out at the night-scape.

The sky was a deep indigo, and she glimpsed the faint pinprick of stars high in the galaxy. Soon they'd begin to fade in a prelude to the encroaching dawn.

Something moved at the peripheral edge of her vision, and she focused on the light, identifying it as a small jet plane *en route* to Coolangatta Airport some thirty kilometres south.

Apartment high-rise buildings stood like tall sentinels, mostly unlit, apart from the occasional window. Street-lights illuminated the main thoroughfare leading to and from central Surfer's Paradise, and there was an occasional glimpse of bright red and green neon.

Traffic was minimal at this hour, and she watched as one crazy motorist raced another on the main road, only to be pursued by a police car with its red and blue lights flashing and siren wailing.

Young hoons risking a drag race, caught up in the adrenalin rush...only to incur a massive fine, loss of licence, and a police record.

'Unable to sleep?'

She'd been so engrossed in the scene below she hadn't heard or sensed his presence. 'I woke up thirsty and came out to get a drink. Did I disturb you?'

More than you know, Jared allowed silently. 'I was awake.'

Tasha didn't say anything for several seconds, then she offered, 'It's so peaceful at this hour.'

He was close, much too close, and she wanted to move away…except her limbs refused to obey the dictates of her brain.

She was aware of him, the faint muskiness lingering from his cologne, his body heat, and his potent masculinity. He slept naked, and she had no trouble envisaging his image, the powerful musculature, his arousal.

Her body swayed a little, almost as if it had a mind of its own, acutely sensitised and receptive to the primitive energy existent between them.

Please, she begged silently. Turn and walk away. I don't think I could bear for you to stay.

She was like a finely tuned instrument, waiting for a master's touch to release the music of her soul. To mesh with his and become something so bewitchingly magical it had the power to rob her of breath, sanity.

She felt the touch of his hands as they cupped her shoulders, and her body sighed, then began to respond.

The fine hairs on her skin lifted, seeking his caress, and emotion curled round her nerve-ends, tugging them into vibrant life.

Jared didn't move, and neither did she. It was almost as if they were teetering on the brink, each afraid to say or do anything to break the spell.

Tasha felt his breath stir the hair at her temples, followed by the fleeting touch of his lips.

His fingers lightly brushed aside a swathe of hair, baring her nape, and sensation spiralled deep within as he pressed his mouth to the curve of her neck, then trailed a light path to tease an earlobe.

She should tell him to stop; and she should take the few steps to move away from him.

Except she stayed, held by a primeval alchemy she found impossible to resist.

A kiss, she told herself. Just…one kiss.

He turned her gently to face him and slid his hands to cup her face, then his mouth closed over hers in a tender supplication that brought a lump to her throat.

His tongue stroked hers, then curved to tease its edge from stem to tip in a persuasive dance, and she felt her bones begin to melt.

The tips of her fingers brushed his shoulders in a light tactile exploration, only to withdraw as if afraid of the heat as his mouth began an evocative exploration…taking, giving, until she was helpless. *His.*

It wasn't enough. It would never be enough, and she groaned as his hand slid down to caress her hip, then slipped to her thigh to skim the bare skin as he pushed up the hem of her nightshirt.

He adored the silky feel of her skin, it was so firm and smooth, and warm to his touch. Sensitive, just inside her hip bone, the indentation at the edge of her waist. He felt the slight tremor run through her body as his hand trailed low and teased the curls at the apex of her thighs. A husky moan escaped her lips when he explored the moistness, the satin cleft, and she sank in against him as he stroked the swollen clitoris.

With one careful movement he pulled the nightshirt over her head and let it fall on the carpet, then he closed his mouth over hers in passionate possession.

When he released her she could only look at him, lost in a sea of emotions so deep, so incredibly complex, it was all she could do not to cry out.

With deliberate intent Jared cupped her bottom, then spread her thighs as he lifted her up against him.

'I don't think—'

'Don't,' he bade huskily, *'think.'* He buried his mouth in the sweet curve of her neck, savoured the sensitive pulse beating there, then he trailed a hand up her spine to cup her nape and caressed her mouth with evocative slowness.

It was a flagrant seduction, and she told herself she didn't care. She wanted this, needed to be swept away by the magic of his lovemaking.

One night, just this one night. Was it so bad to want him so much?

His mouth lifted, and she buried her face in the hollow at the edge of his neck, afraid of what he might see as he walked towards the bedroom.

His bedroom, where moonlight streamed through the non-reflective glass, outlining the furniture, the large bed where he carefully laid her down before joining her there.

'Jared—'

He pressed a finger to the centre of her lower lip, then traced its soft fullness.

'I want to pleasure you,' he said gently, and her mouth quivered as his mouth trailed a path to her breast, savouring the tender peak before rendering a similar treatment to its twin.

Heat arced through her body as he moved lower, and her eyes shimmered with unshed tears as he pressed a series of open-mouthed kisses at her waist, her stomach, before moving low, intent on bestowing the most intimate kiss of all.

At the first stroke of his tongue she went up in flames, spiralling high again and again, until she shattered as ecstasy overwhelmed her.

Her skin was damp, heated as she reached for him, pushing his hands aside as she began a tasting feast that had the breath hissing through his teeth.

There was only one way this could end, and she took him to the brink, then exulted in his possession, the long, slow thrusts as he took her on an evocative ride that was electrifying, mesmeric.

Magical, she added dreamily a long time later as she lay held close in his arms, their limbs entwined, on the edge of sleep.

The room was lighter as night turned into day with a new dawn. Soon the sun would rise above the horizon, gently flooding everything with light and colour as the city woke and came alive.

Tasha's eyelids swept down as she buried her head against Jared's shoulder and slept.

It was late when she woke. Ten, at least, she decided, too lazy to roll over and check the digital clock.

She stretched a little, a purely feline movement, and brushed her foot against a hard, muscular leg. She froze for a second, then memory kicked in, and she turned her head to meet Jared's gleaming gaze.

CHAPTER NINE

'YOU slept well.'

Tasha opened her mouth to say she always slept well after sex, then she closed it again.

He lifted a hand and brushed gentle fingers down her cheek. His mouth curved into a warm smile that was wholly sensual. 'What we shared was beautiful.'

She swallowed the sudden lump in her throat. 'Great sex,' she managed to accord lightly, and saw his eyes darken.

'More than that. Much more.'

She wanted to agree with him, but the words wouldn't emerge. 'I'll go shower.' She had to return to the prosaic, otherwise she'd say something stupid. 'Do you want to eat breakfast in, or shall we go out?'

It didn't work. The pulse beating rapidly at the edge of her throat was a give-away, and her breathing was uneven at best.

This close he was too much. Way too much. Her recollection of last night was hauntingly vivid, and she could still *feel* the effects of his possession.

And worse, there was a part of her that wanted him again. Madness, she derided silently. Total insanity.

He'd seen her naked a thousand times…more, if she was counting. So why was she suddenly reticent about slipping from the bed and walking into the *en suite*?

Oh, damn self-consciousness, she cursed, and did it anyway.

She turned the water dial in the shower to warm, then stood beneath the spray, gradually increasing the temperature before reaching for the soap.

Only to give a surprised yelp as Jared stepped into the cubicle and took the soap from her hand.

'Go away,' she spat fiercely as he began smoothing the soap down the length of her arm.

'Not a chance.'

She put the palm of each hand on his chest and pushed…except it made not the slightest difference. He was immovable.

'Jared—' Her voice became momentarily locked in her throat as he ran the soap over her breast, and his eyes sharpened at her involuntary flinch.

'I hurt you?'

'I…' Oh, hell. She closed her eyes, then opened them again. 'They've become extra-sensitive.'

He held a vivid memory of suckling there, teasing the tender peaks with the edge of his teeth as he took her to the brink between pleasure and pain.

His husky curse was barely audible as he fastened his mouth on hers in a brief, hard kiss before continuing his ministrations.

'Don't.' Tasha curled one hand into a fist and

aimed it at his shoulder as he reached the juncture between her thighs.

He paused, then straightened and met her troubled gaze.

'Last night…' Dammit. 'Just because we had sex, it doesn't mean anything has been resolved.'

Jared stilled, and his expression became an enigmatic mask. 'You call what we shared just…*sex*?'

It was more than that, much more. 'I'd prefer not to discuss it.'

'Avoiding the issue won't make it go away,' Jared warned, and her chin tilted as she held his gaze.

'Any more than you'll allow me to forget it.'

A muscle bunched at the edge of his jaw. 'Take that as a given.'

Tasha turned away from him. 'If you don't mind, I'd prefer to shower alone.'

Hands curved over her shoulders and he brought her round to face him. 'And if I do mind?'

Anger lent her eyes a fiery sparkle. 'Tough.'

His mouth covered hers, hard and possessively demanding as he tore her initial resistance to shreds.

She balled one hand into a fist and took aim, uncaring where she connected, only to cry out as he took hold of her hand and clamped it behind her back, then brought the other to join it in a movement that succeeded in bringing her up against him.

He held her easily, quelling any struggle she attempted as he slid his other hand to her nape, and he angled his head, using the strength of his jaw to force open her mouth.

She made a sound deep in her throat that was part groan, part entreaty, and after a few timeless seconds he wrenched his mouth from hers.

Tasha wasn't capable of saying a word. Her lips, her tongue felt numb from his invasion, and he released her with a sound of self-disgust.

Tears rose to the surface, shimmered there, and she blinked in an effort to prevent their spill.

Firm fingers caught hold of her chin, lifting it so she had no recourse but to look at him, and she swiftly lowered her lashes in an effort to hide the pain of his violation.

His husky oath was indistinguishable, and she stiffened as he traced a gentle finger over the swollen contours of her mouth.

'Go,' Jared adjured quietly. 'Before I do or say something totally regrettable.'

She didn't need second bidding, and she stepped out of the shower stall, caught up a towel, wrapped it round her slender curves and escaped into the bedroom, where, towelled dry, she donned fresh underwear, stepped into jeans and pulled on a cotton-knit top.

Jared emerged into the bedroom, a towel tucked low over his hips, and Tasha felt the impact of his analytical appraisal. At that precise moment she hated him, so much so it brought on a wave of nauseousness.

She must have paled, for she heard his sharpened demand. 'Tasha?'

Seconds later she made a running dive for the *en suite* and was horribly, violently ill.

He was there, holding her shaking shoulders, stroking the hair back from her face, then when it was over he caught up a face cloth and cleansed her face.

'OK?' he queried gently.

Oh, God. 'I think so.' Morning sickness had reared its head again. With a vengeance, she accorded wryly, and wretched timing.

'Stay here. I'll go make some tea and toast.'

Her stomach roiled at the thought of food. Yet the pregnant mother's manual was big on tea and something light to ease the symptoms.

'I don't think I'm quite done,' she managed a few seconds ahead of a repeat performance.

Jared held her, then cleansed her face again, swearing softly as he caught sight of the tears welling in her eyes.

'Don't.'

It was just reaction, and she told him so as he lightly kissed the moisture from beneath each eye.

'I'll be OK. Just…get me that tea,' she said shakily.

While he was gone she cleaned her teeth, brushed her hair and tied it back, then when Jared returned she sank into a chair and sipped the hot, sweet tea. The slice of toast helped, and by the time she'd finished both tea and toast she felt almost human again.

'Thanks.'

He took the empty cup and plate and placed them on the bedside pedestal.

'How long have you been suffering morning sickness?'

'About a week.'

He stroked gentle fingers down her cheek. 'Do you feel up to a walk along the beach, then breakfast at Tedder Avenue?'

The thought of fresh air and sunshine was a welcome one. 'Yes.'

'Give me five minutes to shave and dress.'

Tasha slid her feet into trainers, fixed the laces, then she collected the cup and plate and took them out to the kitchen.

Jared joined her there, and together they rode the lift down to the lobby, then stepped out onto the expanse of sand.

He caught hold of her hand and threaded his fingers through her own. She wanted to remain angry with him for that punishing kiss in the shower. Except somehow his caring for her afterwards negated any feeling of animosity.

It was a lovely morning, the sun's warmth caressed her skin as a soft ocean breeze teased a few loose tendrils of her hair. The smell of the sea was subtle, just a drift in the air, and Tasha lifted her face to catch it as they wandered towards Narrow Neck, then turned and retraced their steps.

Breakfast became brunch, and afterwards they returned to the apartment to pick up their overnight bags, then Jared headed the car towards the mountains, taking the steep, winding gradient up to Mount Tamborine, where they stopped at one of several roadside cafés for tea and scones before browsing the crafts and wares.

Tasha bought some homemade jam and a cute little pottery cat, then they took the road through Canungra and onto the northern motorway, reaching Brisbane just before dark.

'Shall we settle for pizza or Chinese?' Jared queried as the Brisbane river came into view.

'Pizza.'

'Take-out, or eat in?'

'You're giving me a choice?'

'Of course.'

She thought of red-checked tablecloths, empty Chianti bottles with lit candles, the redolent aroma of spices and garlic bread, and didn't hesitate in naming an upmarket pizzeria in suburban Milton.

It was a very pleasant way to end the day, and she selected her favoured capriccioso while Jared settled for one loaded with salami, olives and sun-dried tomatoes.

Heaven, Tasha decided as she finished one slice and reached for another.

'You're due to appear in court tomorrow.' A well-publicised rape case which promised to be a media circus. 'Are you happy with the jury selection?' Something that was often a long and arduous process before the defence and prosecuting legal representatives were satisfied.

'Yes.'

It was a definitive answer, and she knew only too well the long hours he'd devoted to the case, the research involved. 'Who is the presiding judge?'

Jared named him, and her eyebrows rose a little. Well-respected, the judge was nevertheless known in legal circles for his tough stance on certain issues, and rape was one of them.

The facts were indisputable, the evidence weighted very strongly in favour of the victim. However, she was aware one of Jared's highly skilled colleagues had been engaged as defence.

'A clash of the titans,' she observed lightly. It was an unnecessary question, but she asked it anyway. 'Soleil is in on the case?'

'Her father offered me the brief,' Jared drawled, and she inclined her head.

'Of course,' she acknowledged wryly.

'Cynicism doesn't suit you.'

'She wants you,' she posed with pseudo-sweetness.

'While I see her only as an associate.'

'Albeit a very attractive one.'

He regarded her quizzically. 'You want me to deny that?'

'And lie to me?'

A husky chuckle emerged from his throat. 'Are you going to finish that pizza?'

'Don't change the subject.'

The exchange of light banter brought forth memories of other occasions when they'd stopped off for pizza after a lazy Sunday. Except then when the meal was over they'd drive home, share the spa and indulge in a glass of wine, before making love long into the night.

Tonight, however, would have a different ending, and she experienced a twinge of sadness as Jared drew the car to a halt outside the entrance to her Kangaroo Point apartment.

'If I ask you to collect a few changes of clothes and come back with me,' Jared posed quietly, 'will you refuse?'

Did he know just how much she wanted to do that? To go back to where they were ten days ago? But there was the thing…you couldn't turn back the clock. You could only go forward.

'I—don't think that's a good idea.'

'Because you don't want to? Or you can't?'

'Both.'

'You know I won't leave it there?'

She chose not to answer as she released her seat belt and opened the door. 'I'll just collect my bag.'

He doused the lights and switched off the engine.

'There's no need to get out.'

'Don't be ridiculous.' He reached into the back seat and retrieved her overnight bag.

'Thanks,' Tasha said seconds later as they reached the entrance. She used her key to open the outer door and took hold of her bag. 'Goodnight.'

CHAPTER TEN

JARED rang just before eight as she was finishing her second cup of tea.

'How did you fare this morning?'

Tasha endeavoured to ignore the way her pulse leapt at the sound of Jared's voice. 'A repeat of yesterday.'

'That bad, huh?'

She wanted to say *yes*, and it's all your fault. Except it wasn't his fault any more than it was hers.

'I'll be fine.' She'd be even better if she wasn't bent on doing this alone.

'I'll call you tonight.'

Tasha disconnected the call, then headed for the shower.

The following few days were hectic, with work consuming most of Tasha's waking hours. She went in to the office early, and took paperwork home, often not closing her laptop until late. Only to repeat the procedure all over again.

Jared was similarly caught up with the current case in hand, and he phoned each day, usually in the morning from his chambers before she left for the city.

It came as no surprise when he rang Wednesday

morning just as she was putting the finishing touches to her make-up, and she kept her tone brisk.

'I'm about to walk out the door.'

'So keep it brief?'

'Please.'

'I have to fly down to Melbourne tomorrow morning for a mediation meeting.'

'Is Soleil going with you?'

'Yes.'

Wonderful. 'Have fun,' she managed lightly, and heard the mild exasperation in his voice as he said, 'I'll ring when I get back.'

'There's no need,' she said stiffly. She'd tried for 'nice' and failed. Soleil had that effect on her.

It didn't sit well Soleil was accompanying him to Melbourne, no matter how she qualified it was business and they'd be on the evening flight back to Brisbane.

Instinct did much to assure Soleil's innuendo was based on wishful thinking. Yet there were sufficient facts woven in with the lies to cast doubt.

Strong feelings, even stronger emotions had roused her temper, and it wasn't done yet.

'Have a good trip, a successful day.' The words held little more than formal politeness. Angry with herself, *him,* she cut the call.

It was as well the day was a hectic one, for there was little or no time to think. A lunch break became something she sacrificed in lieu of a sandwich snatched between seeing clients, supplemented by fruit, ditto.

She stayed late, took work home, and retired later than she should have, only to wake at dawn unable to get back to sleep.

It didn't help to have Jared's image rise up and taunt her, or for the way her mind seemed bent on reflection.

Her doubt had centred around his perspective, his long-term commitment, and not wanting to force the issue of marriage if he hadn't wanted the legality of it.

Yet in the past few weeks nothing had changed, except the changes she herself had made.

At what point would he relinquish the relationship and resign himself to being a single father?

Worse, move on to another relationship?

It wasn't as if there weren't any number of women only too willing to step into her shoes! Soleil was merely one of many.

The thought she might lose him filled her with fear.

Dammit, she couldn't just lie here and stew. She'd go make some tea, nibble a slice of toast, boot up her laptop and work until it was time to shower and dress, and go into the office.

Tonight, she'd call Jared and suggest they meet and attempt to reconcile their differences. There really wasn't any other way…for her. And she clung to the hope it was the same for him.

The day became a replica of the preceding one, with a staff shortfall and urgent work redistributed.

It proved a welcome distraction, and she entered

her apartment at six, fixed a healthy chicken salad and ate it as she browsed through the day's newspaper.

When she finished she dealt with the dishes, filled a glass with chilled water, then she crossed to the lounge and switched on the television.

The news was running, and she stood engrossed in an update on a worsening crisis in the Middle East. The picture disappeared, the newsreader picked up an updated bulletin and began reading as the tele-monitor ran a newsflash across the lower edge of the screen.

Bomb explosion at Melbourne's Tullamarine Airport. Seven dead, several injured. Domestic terminal evacuated and all flights cancelled until further notice.

Did stomachs plummet? Hearts stop? Tasha felt as if she experienced both in succession.

Jared. Ohmigod, *Jared*. She felt as if she couldn't breathe, and she fought against the terror as she raced to the phone.

If he was OK, he'd have rung from his cell-phone. Somehow the fact he hadn't only heightened her fear.

Except she had his number on speed dial, and she tried it first. Just in case. Only to receive the 'out of range' signal. Maybe he'd switched it off prior to boarding. She sent an SMS text message, and waited anxiously for a response, but none came.

There had to be an emergency number set up for direct enquiries. The television station would screen it, and she flicked from channel to channel before she discovered the newsflash, then began dialling.

There was no indication of the passage of time as her call was dealt with, particulars patiently taken, a seemingly interminable wait while the operator checked available details.

'We have no one of that name listed among the injured,' the operator confirmed, then offered quietly, 'Please check back in an hour.'

Tasha knew she'd go mad if she had to wait an hour, but she had no recourse other than to sit by the phone as she watched newsflash updates via television.

Jared has to be alive. He has to be OK.

The words kept echoing through her brain like a mantra. After a while she began doing deals with the deity.

One clear fact emerged. Life without Jared would be no life at all.

It was something she'd known all along, yet she had stupidly clung to principles…principles which now meant nothing.

Tasha gazed sightlessly at images on the television screen, and only jerked into full alert when the latest newsflash showed.

Five minutes before the hour was up she redialled the emergency number, only to wait in line until her call could be answered by an operative.

Ten minutes later she was told Jared's name did not appear on their growing list of identified injured.

There was an overriding need to board a flight and go there in person. As if that would do any good. But at least she'd be *there*.

Oh, dear God. If anything happened to him, she'd die.

The sudden peal of her cell-phone didn't register for a millisecond, then she snatched it up with shaking fingers and activated the call.

'Tasha.'

The sound of Jared's voice sent her into a tailspin, and she clutched the phone unit so hard her fingers went numb. 'Are you OK?' She hardly recognised her own voice; it was so choked the words were almost indistinguishable.

'A scratch or two from flying debris.' He wouldn't reveal how luck had played a part, or just how close he'd come to serious injury. 'The medics insisted we all be transported to hospital. My cell-phone died. This is the first chance I had to get to a phone. We'll be accommodated overnight, flights are being rescheduled from another airport. I'll phone as soon as I have further details.' He paused fractionally, then added quietly, 'I love you.'

Tasha swallowed the lump in her throat, and wanted to weep as the connection was cut.

How could he say that, then hang up? Leave her literally gasping for air at a time when she'd just come out of a ragged few hours when she imagined he could be severely injured or worse?

Restless, too much so to *sit*, she sought physical activity in the form of house-cleaning. Not that the apartment needed much, but she directed her energies into removing every speck of dust and buffing everything to a gleaming shine.

It was after ten when she finished, and she opted for a shower, then bed. Would Jared ring again tonight? Unlikely, given Melbourne was on summer daylight-saving time and an hour ahead of Brisbane.

Sleep didn't come easily, and she twisted and turned in bed, punched her pillow countless times, then gave up in disgust and padded out to the lounge to sit curled up in a chair watching late-night television.

It was dawn when she stirred, and she crept into bed to sleep until the alarm woke her. She checked her cell-phone, but there were no text messages, and she showered, ate cereal and fruit for breakfast and washed it down with tea, then she dressed ready for work.

Her emotions were in an ambivalent state, swinging from nervous anticipation to excitement, then dipping to doubt as the morning progressed.

At ten her cell-phone buzzed with an incoming text message, and she counted off the seconds until the message registered before hurriedly accessing it.

'Returning late-afternoon flight. Be ready 7 pm. We'll dine out'.

Tasha quickly text messaged back 'OK'.

Thank heavens. Relief washed through her body, followed by slow, tingling warmth.

With conscious effort she focused on the day's work, took and kept appointments, and willed the hours to pass.

During her lunch break she visited a nearby florist and purchased a single red rose.

At five she shut her laptop, collected her briefcase, and walked out to the bank of lifts. Given peak-hour traffic, she should reach her apartment within half an hour.

She made it in less, and headed straight for the shower, washed and blow-dried her hair, then dressed with care, choosing an elegant black lace dress with a scooped neckline, elbow-length sleeves and a hemline halting an inch above the knee. Black stilettos, minimum jewellery, and skilled use of make-up completed the outfit, then she caught up an evening purse, the long-stemmed rose, and exited the apartment.

Jared's image was a constant, and the nerves inside her stomach went from a slow waltz to an energetic tango as she took the lift down to the lobby.

It was precisely seven when she emerged on the ground floor, and she saw Jared standing beside his car waiting for her.

Within seconds she reached his side, her gaze raking his features for any visible sign of injury.

'Where are you hurt?' It was the most pressing question she had, and surpassed 'hello' by a mile.

He tunnelled his fingers through her hair and lowered his head to hers to take possession of her mouth in a kiss that was hard, hot and hungry. Then he eased off and went back for more, this time with a gentleness that melted her bones.

Tasha felt the need to touch him, to hold on and never let go, and she sank in against him, loving the physical feel of him, knowing he was flesh and blood, *alive*.

'Are you really OK?'

His lips brushed her cheek, then settled at the edge of her mouth. 'A couple of scratches, a few bruises. I was one of the lucky ones.'

'Thank God,' she said with undue reverence, and saw his mouth curve into a warm, musing smile.

'My sentiments, exactly.'

She had to ask. 'Soleil?'

'A broken arm, several fractured ribs. She's staying in Melbourne until she feels sufficiently comfortable to travel.'

She touched the hard planes of his face, lingered there, then traced the curve of his mouth, and caught her breath as he pressed a warm kiss to her palm.

'I take it you want to eat?'

His teasing query brought forth a smile. 'I am hungry.' For food, as well as you, she added silently. But the waiting wouldn't go amiss, and anticipation was good for the soul.

He threaded his fingers through her own, then moved to open the passenger door, waiting until she was seated before crossing round to slide in behind the wheel.

The restaurant was situated in the suburbs, distant

from the trendy boutique restaurants populated by the city's café society.

Tasha doubted she'd ever been quite so nervous, and she wondered if Jared was aware her pulse was racing at a rapid beat.

Her heart felt as if it was thundering against her ribcage as they entered the softly lit interior. The *maitre d'* greeted them, she gave her name, and then preceded Jared to their table.

She set the rose down, then slid into the seat the waiter held out for her.

Jared indicated the delicate red bud on the tablecloth. 'I assume this has some special significance?'

'Yes.'

Did her hands shake as she perused the menu? She hoped not. Cool, calm, collected, she reminded silently.

Her gaze strayed to his elegant suit, and saw the male frame beneath it. The powerful musculature in those broad shoulders, the taut midriff, trim waist, lean hips, and…better not go there, she decided shakily. She was in such an emotionally fragile state any thought of his sexual prowess would bring her undone.

She was way too nervous to eat, and she ordered a small salad as a starter and followed it with an entrée-size main.

'Was the mediation meeting successful?'

Jared cast her a piercing look. 'I'm pleased with the way it went.'

Polite, she was being way too polite. Oh, what in

hell was the matter with her? Confidence had subtly changed to doubt, she acknowledged silently.

Yet the same stubborn resolve which had been responsible for her moving out of his apartment had motivated her to pose a question.

Sure, she mentally derided as she refused dessert and ordered tea. But would he say *yes*?

Except she'd come this far, and she wasn't about to wimp out.

Now, do it now, an inner voice commanded.

It took only seconds to retrieve the carefully written card from her evening bag. She met Jared's gaze with deliberate equanimity as she transferred the rose onto the table beside his plate and added the card.

'A gift,' she offered in explanation. For him, only him. The gift of herself and their unborn child.

Would he accept? Dear lord, she hoped so. A cold hand clutched hold of her heart, and squeezed.

Even thinking of rejection sent her tumbling into a downward spiral towards emotional despair.

There was nothing evident in his expression to indicate his reaction. She'd expected quizzical amusement, maybe a few bantering words in response.

She knew the words by heart. She'd used up a few cards getting the words right.

You are the love of my life. Will you marry me?

She waited, the breath locked in her throat. How long did it take for him to read the words? Assimilate...*answer* them?

It seemed forever before he lifted his head and met her gaze. 'Is there anything you want to add?'

Tasha swallowed painfully. 'This isn't because of the child. It's about *you*.' She gathered courage, and tried to ignore the way her fingers worked the linen napkin on her lap, pleating and re-pleating it in sheer nervousness. 'About not being trapped into something you didn't want,' she said quietly.

'Am I to surmise you don't think that any more?'

How could she? When the lovemaking had been so exquisite, so soul-shattering it had been all she could do not to splinter into a thousand pieces. 'Yes.'

Was she aware of the impact such a simple word had on him? How he'd suffered these past few weeks, wanting, needing, *aching* for her? Unable, helpless to do anything about it?

He hadn't had a decent night's sleep since she moved out of his apartment. The world, as he knew it, had turned upside-down and become a place he didn't want to be if she wasn't there with him.

He looked at her, saw the woman she was, what she'd become…her strengths, values, her integrity. And knew that he'd never take her for granted again. Love was a gift, given from the heart.

'Are you going to tell me what changed your mind?'

So many things, but she revealed the most important of all. 'You could have walked away, but you didn't,' she continued simply. Was that her voice? It sounded impossibly husky.

Something shifted in his eyes, a momentary darkness she couldn't define. 'Not entirely alone.'

She retained a vivid memory of their night together at the Gold Coast when passion had overcome them both.

Tasha managed a slight musing smile. 'No.'

He hadn't given her an answer. Was he stalling? Putting off the moment when he would regretfully decline?

Dear heaven. He couldn't…wouldn't…*No*. The word was a silent scream of despair. The ache of unshed tears filled her eyes, dimming her vision.

'I love you.' Her mouth shook a little, and she sought for control. 'Only you.' Oh, God, she was going to lose it completely. 'When news of the bomb blast broke…the thought you might have died…' She couldn't continue for a few seconds, then she took a deep breath and released it. 'My life would be worth nothing without you.'

Something sighed deep within, effecting a subtle shift in his emotional heart as everything fell into place. The blood coursed through his veins, sang a little.

He'd almost lost her. Thought for a while that he had. Yet he'd fought back, aware nothing came with any guarantees…not even love.

The most precious gift of all, beyond price.

He leant forward and trailed his fingers along the curve of her cheek. 'Yes.'

Yes? Did he mean—?

'I accept your proposal.'

Relief, elation were only two of the immediate emotions she experienced, and he watched as her expressive features lit with a joy so intense it made his heart ache.

'Soon,' Jared added softly. 'Very soon.' He wanted his ring on her finger, not as proof of his ownership, but as visible evidence they belonged to each other.

The waiter appeared at their table and laid a red rose on the tablecloth. 'For you, ma'am.' He cast Jared a smile. 'From your gentleman.'

She was so touched by the gesture she had to fight to hold back the shimmer of tears, and she picked up the rose and admired the soft velvet-like petals curving protectively layer upon layer in perfect symmetry.

'Two minds,' Jared said gently, indicating the rose she'd placed on the table earlier. 'In perfect accord.'

'It's beautiful,' she murmured, and absently stroked the bud with a forefinger. The delicate perfume was much sought-after by the world's top perfumeries, and she could understand why.

Jared summoned immense will-power in order to prevent himself from hauling her into his arms. 'Let's get out of here.'

Her gaze shifted to lock with his, and her eyes darkened at what she saw reflected in those mesmerising depths. 'You haven't finished your coffee.'

He summoned the waiter, settled the bill, then led Tasha out to the car.

She threaded her fingers through his own, and didn't relinquish them as they reached the Jaguar. There was just one last thing she wanted to say, and the words came easily as she met his dark enquiring gaze.

'You let me go. Allowed me time and space alone. I want to thank you for that.'

'It was the hardest thing I've ever had to do.'

But worth it, he assured silently, to have what they now shared...no doubts, no shadows. Just everything he'd hoped, prayed for—and prayer wasn't one of his strong points, except he'd been so desperate he'd have resorted to anything that might give him an edge.

He held her close, and adored the way she sank in against him. They were so completely in tune, so much a part of each other, he could only reflect with regret how he'd loved and cherished her, but had been so far entrenched in a comfort zone he'd neglected to provide the reassurance she needed.

'Your place, or mine?' It was one or the other.

She spared him a musing look as he opened the car door for her. 'Your choice.'

'Mine,' Jared said with satisfaction as the car sped towards the city. 'It's where you belong.'

And where she'd stay. He'd make sure of it. Not that it was the *where* that mattered, as long as she was with him for the rest of his life.

Jared drove with controlled care, the image of her sharing his bed...beneath him, her moist heat, the way her eyes went blank the moment she climaxed. It was enough to almost suspend his breathing.

He reached the underground car park and felt a measure of satisfaction at the faint squeal of rubber on concrete as he eased the Jaguar into its allotted space.

They both slid out at the same time, and joined hands *en route* to the lift. He lifted her hand to his lips during the rapid ascent, and almost drowned in the liquid warmth evident...her soft smile, the almost tremulous quiver of her mouth. A mouth he intended to take with his own the instant they were inside his apartment.

They barely made it. Tasha wanted the feel of skin on skin, the warmth, the heat and heart of him, and she wanted it now.

She slid her hands inside his jacket and pushed it over his shoulders, then her fingers tore at the buttons on his shirt, pulled it free from his trousers, and went for snap, the zip fastener.

Oh, dear heaven, his clean scent was heady like potent wine, and she savoured it with her lips, her tongue, running from shoulder to chest, where she teased the hair curling there, then laved a male nipple before sliding lower.

Jared hauled her up against him, and she wound her legs around his waist, then angled her mouth against his and took him deep, plundering until he held fast her head and savaged her mouth in a hard, hungry kiss that was nowhere near enough to slake their need.

It became his turn to dispense with her clothes, and he did so with economy of movement, then feasted on her breast, suckling, using the edge of his teeth to take her to the brink between pleasure and pain.

The bedroom. The bed. He wanted both, and he made his way there, tumbling her onto the mattress and following her down.

The rest of their clothes were tossed onto the carpet, and his fingers sought the moist heart of her, stroked, then dug deep and felt her go up and over as she groaned his name.

'Please. Now.'

He entered her slowly, relished her slick heat, and the breath husked from his throat as she enclosed him, moved with him as he set the rhythm, urging a pace he consciously controlled to a lesser degree.

It was good. Dear heaven, it was better than *good*.

Afterwards he supported his body above her own, and trailed his lips across her forehead, lingered at one temple, then began the slow slide down her cheek, paused at the edge of her mouth, traced its curve, and settled in a slow, erotic open-mouthed kiss that almost made her weep.

'Not fair,' Tasha murmured, and pushed him to lie on his back as she straddled him.

'Want to play, huh?'

His eyes gleamed as she bent low and nipped at the curve between his neck and shoulder.

'My turn.' She wanted to taste him, absorb his

essence…most of all, she wanted to drive him wild. With want, need, and desire for her. Only her.

She succeeded, with each indrawn breath, each hiss between clenched teeth, a husky groan adding to her euphoria.

There was a tremendous sense of power in pleasuring a man. Taking him to a place where he was no longer in control and completely at her mercy.

The ultimate in surrender. Absolute trust. Man at his most vulnerable.

She loved the way his stomach quivered at her touch, the clench of muscles as her lips teased and tantalised.

It became a glorious sensual feast from which they both emerged satisfied, sated, and emotionally spent.

They slept for a while, then woke through the night and sought each other again. And again.

It wasn't enough, would never be enough, and as the sun rose above the horizon Jared carried her into the *en suite*, ran the shower, then stepped into the large cubicle and picked up the soap.

Tasha simply closed her eyes and went with the intimate luxury of having him administer to her.

He was so incredibly gentle it almost made her weep, and she swayed slightly as his hand splayed over her stomach and lingered there.

When he was done, she took the soap from him and returned the favour, her eyes narrowing as she glimpsed bruises forming over his ribs, the edge of one shoulder, on the curve of his hip.

'Turn around.' When he didn't budge, she stepped round behind him and examined his back, found evidence of more bruising, and gritted her teeth. 'You should have told me.' A soft curse fell from her lips. 'Dammit, Jared. You should have been more careful when we—'

'I didn't feel a thing at the time.'

His voice held humour, and she lightly slapped his butt. 'I love it when you get physical.' He reached out and closed the water dial, then his eyes darkened as he felt the press of her lips against one bruise, and he stood still as she gently caressed each bruise in turn.

When she reached the last, he hauled her close and kissed her with infinite tenderness. Then he caught up a towel and gently dried her before applying the towel to himself.

He carried her back to bed, curled her in close, and pulled up the covers.

CHAPTER ELEVEN

THEY rose late, dressed, and went into the kitchen to cook breakfast. Jared took care of the eggs, bacon and hash-browns, while Tasha tended to the toast, tea and coffee.

There was no rush, and they took their time, sampling toast, offering each other a succulent piece of bacon, then lingered over tea and coffee.

Together they cleared the table, rinsed dishes and stacked them in the dishwasher.

'There's something I want to show you.'

Tasha closed the dishwasher and turned towards him. Attired in jeans and a black T-shirt, he looked ruggedly attractive and vaguely piratical. Absent was the formality of a barrister at law, and her stomach executed a slow somersault at the way the T-shirt emphasised his muscular breadth of shoulder.

She had a vivid memory of how she'd clung to him through the night, over and over again, in a sensual dance that had been without equal.

Jared crossed to her side, caught hold of her hand and threaded his fingers through her own. 'Let's go.'

She lifted her face to his, saw the purposeful gleam apparent, and offered a warm laugh. 'Do I get to ask *where*?'

He bestowed a brief, hard kiss to her mouth, then softened it with a slow sweep of his tongue. 'No.' He led her into the lounge, collected his keys and slid them into his pocket. 'I want it to be a surprise.'

'OK.'

He slanted her a musing smile. 'Just *OK*?'

'You want I should argue?'

His mouth curved, deepening the faint vertical grooves slashing each cheek. 'Sassy, huh?'

She lifted their linked hands to her mouth and brushed his knuckles with her lips. 'Happy,' she declared quietly. 'And so in love with you.'

Jared paused in reaching for the door, and drew her into his arms. His lips touched her temple, then trailed to the edge of her mouth, savoured the sensual curve and absorbed the sound of his name as it rose from her throat.

A hand slid beneath her hair, cupping her nape, angling her head as he embarked on an evocative tasting that left her weak-willed and yearning.

He released her slowly, and his eyes darkened as she ran the edge of her tongue over her lower lip.

'If we don't get out of here, I doubt we'll make it at all,' Tasha opined shakily.

Without a word Jared reached out and opened the door, and they crossed the foyer to the bank of lifts, where one took them down to the basement carpark.

Jared set the Jaguar across the bridge spanning the river, and drove through the city to suburban Ascot.

Late spring saw many gardens bursting with flowers, their colours varying from a wild, unplanned mix to sculptured colour-co-ordinated beds carefully tended by an expert's hand. Neat mown lawns, symmetrical topiary, and clipped shrubbery.

A delightful suburb, with beautiful tree-lined avenues, spacious older homes, some of which were set in their original grounds and occupied by second- and third-generation families.

There were also the newer residences, built of brick and stone, cement-rendered, modern, with floor-to-ceiling glass the better to view the river and inner harbour.

Tasha was intrigued when Jared turned off the main road circling the river and began an ascending gradient that took them high onto the hill.

'I'm not exactly dressed for visiting anyone,' she began cautiously, aware of her jeans and top, and he offered a warm smile.

'You're fine as you are,' he assured as he accessed an avenue, drove a hundred metres, then turned into a curved driveway.

The house stood well back in large, spacious grounds, and it was all she could do not to breathe an appreciative sigh as she admired its gracious lines, the verandas framing the east and west sides. French doors, shutters…a beautiful blend of stunning architecture.

The only thing blotting such perfection was a cavernous hole in the grounds, and a mound of builders' supplies which indicated interior renovations together with the addition of a swimming pool.

The view was fantastic, and would hold an even wider scope from any of the upstairs windows. Although she doubted she'd have the opportunity to see it.

Jared drew the car to a halt and released his seat belt. 'Let's go in, shall we?'

Tasha followed suit and slid to her feet. There was a gentle breeze, the air crisp and clean, and she caught the drift of scented roses from a manicured rose-bed near by.

'Are we expected?' It was Saturday, mid-morning. The owners could be out, or perhaps ferrying children to a sports activity.

At that moment the double front door opened and a middle-aged couple stood framed in the aperture.

'Mr North.'

Mr North seemed formal, unless they were clients. Which hardly made sense, when this was supposedly a social call.

'Amy and Joe Falconer. Tasha Peterson.' Jared performed the introduction. 'Amy and Joe are live-in caretakers until the renovations are completed.'

Disbelief was replaced by incredulity as she searched his features. 'This is your house?' Pleasure lent a sparkle to her eyes. 'You bought it?'

'Yes. Let's go indoors and explore.' He placed a hand on her shoulder. 'You can tell me if you like it.'

Large rooms, polished floors, high ceilings... She moved from room to room, loving the open fireplace, the spaciousness, the wide curved staircase leading to the upper floor.

'What's not to like?'

Delight was evident in her expression, and he curved an arm around her shoulders as they ascended the stairs.

Tasha listened to his plans as he led her along a wide central hallway. 'The bedroom next to the master bedroom is being turned into a nursery,' he outlined, indicating the partly finished structural changes. 'And the two rooms on this side will become a study and law library.'

There were three remaining bedrooms, two of which connected to an *en suite*, and a larger room with its own *en suite*.

'What do you think?'

'It's beautiful,' she said with heartfelt sincerity.

'The decorators are due to start the week after next. I want you to have an input in the colour scheme. Then there's furniture and furnishings.'

He had everything in hand, and that took some planning. 'When did you buy the house?' She told herself it didn't matter, that knowing was merely a curiosity factor.

'I've had my eye on it for some time.'

'That doesn't answer the question.'

He grasped both her hands, then slid his own up her arms to close over each shoulder. 'I clinched the deal within days of you telling me you were pregnant.'

'You were that sure of me?'

'I was sure of my own feelings,' he said gently. 'Certain I wanted to be with you for the rest of my life.' He cupped her face, tilted it. 'I just needed to prove it to you.'

She wasn't capable of saying a word.

'There are a couple more things.' He released her and reached into the pocket of his jeans. 'This.' He caught hold of her left hand and slid a ring onto her finger.

This was an exquisitely cut pear-shaped diamond which tore the breath from her throat.

'We have a date with a minister two weeks from today.'

'Two *weeks*?' She could feel her head begin to spin. 'You're joking…aren't you?' She couldn't possibly organise a dress—

'No,' Jared refuted, watching the play of emotions on her expressive features. 'And yes, you can,' he added gently, reading her mind. 'I'll arrange the reception venue, caterers. Just family and close friends. All you need to do is take care of yourself.'

And he did. Calling in favours, arranging everything down to the finest detail.

Tasha enlisted Eloise as her matron of honour, and her life became a whirlwind as they did the bridal boutiques, the couture houses, added lingerie to the list, indulged in a facial, massage, and bought make-up.

'Shop till you drop' was Eloise's favoured *modus operandi*. Add a full work schedule, and each day seemed more hectic than the last. At night Tasha fell asleep in Jared's arms, then rose to repeat the previous day all over again.

'You'll stay with us the night before the wedding,' Eloise declared, only to have Jared issue a rebuttal.

'The hell you will.'

'Don't want to let me out of your sight, huh?'

'Got it in one. Besides, Eloise will keep you up all night talking "girl-talk".'

That was entirely possible, and she offered him a wicked smile. 'I'll tell her to be here at ten.'

'The groom isn't supposed to see the bride on her wedding day until she walks down the aisle,' Eloise protested fiercely when Tasha relayed she'd be leaving for the church from Jared's apartment. 'Don't you *dare* imagine you're riding in the same car to the church.'

'Separate times, different cars,' Tasha vouched.

'That's OK, then. Now,' Eloise continued with unquenchable enthusiasm. 'Let's go through our list again.'

With only one day to go, 'the list' had diminished to a few last-minute essentials. Thank heavens. There had been times when elopement seemed an enviable option.

It was late when she slid into bed, and she sighed as Jared drew her close.

'Relax,' he bade quietly. 'And enjoy.'

He began with her feet, massaging gently, easing out the kinks in her calves, thighs, and she closed her eyes. It was heaven, all of it. A lover's touch.

There was nothing to surpass the blissful release of emotions.

When her breathing became deep and even, he carefully pulled up the bedcovers and settled down beside her, content in the knowledge of what the next day would bring.

Saturday dawned with a sprinkle of rain which cleared by mid-morning, followed by warm sunshine and azure skies.

It was a perfect day for a wedding. Although Tasha wouldn't have cared if the heavens opened and provided a deluge of rain. It was the occasion that held importance, not the weather.

'Nervous?'

She stood still as Eloise fixed the coronet of miniature roses in place.

'No.' There were no doubts, no hidden insecurities. Just a feeling of everything being right.

Eloise pressed the last hairclip in place, then stepped back to admire her handiwork. 'Beautiful,' she complimented gently and met Tasha's smile via mirrored reflection.

'Thanks.'

She'd chosen simplicity over froth and frills for her gown, and the fitted bodice with its scooped neckline, capped sleeves and gently billowing skirt complimented her slender figure.

A single pearl on a delicate gold chain and matching ear-studs completed the image, and her make-up was skilfully minimal.

'OK, sweetheart,' Eloise declared with impish affection. 'Let's get this show on the road.'

Family and close friends were already gathered inside the small stone church when the hired limousine deposited Tasha and Eloise immediately adjacent to the main doors.

Monica stood inside the vestibule, and she stepped forward to give Tasha a reassuring hug. 'I love you.'

Tears shimmered in the woman's eyes, and Tasha felt her own fill with moisture. 'Ditto,' she responded quietly.

'Cool it,' Eloise admonished succinctly. 'Smile now, cry later. Think *happy*.'

'We are,' Tasha and her prospective mother-in-law assured in unison.

'Jared's waiting.'

And he was, standing tall with his back to the altar as he watched his bride step down the aisle.

Tasha saw only him, and her gaze became trapped in his as the congregation faded from her vision. It was as if they were the only two people in the world, and her mouth trembled at the depth of emotion evident in those dark eyes. For her.

Her breath caught in her throat, and she was prepared to swear her heart stopped beating for a few seconds as sheer joy became an overwhelming entity.

She reached him as no other woman ever had, or ever would. Truly beautiful where beauty really mattered…in the heart and soul. It was something he'd never hold back from telling her.

Just as he had no intention of holding back now. To hell with convention and protocol.

Jared lifted his hands and captured her face, then he lowered his head and kissed her…with such lingering thoroughness it almost melted her bones.

'If the bride and groom are ready, perhaps we can begin?'

There was a ripple of amused laughter from the guests, and Tasha whispered, 'This is a serious occasion.'

'I've never been more serious in my life,' Jared reiterated, and brushed his lips to hers for good measure.

The ceremony held a special significance, as did the solemn words binding them together, and afterwards their shared happiness was something to behold, bringing a catch to many a female throat as the evening progressed.

It was almost ten when they took their leave, and used a chauffeured limousine to drive them to Jared's apartment, where they changed into casual clothes, collected overnight bags and took the limousine down to the Gold Coast.

Constraints of work and his appearance in court meant they only had the weekend, and they'd opted for the Main Beach apartment rather than a hotel.

Jared switched on the lights and locked the door as Tasha crossed the lounge and stood looking out at the view through floor-to-ceiling glass.

Tall apartment buildings with various lit windows outlined against an indigo sky. A steady stream of cars traversing the highway with their twin beams of light. The inky blackness of the river flowing out into the open sea.

'Looking at something in particular?' Jared drawled from behind.

She'd sensed rather than heard him cross the room, and she leaned back against him as his arms circled her waist.

'It's beautiful,' she said simply, indicating the night-scape. 'I don't think you could ever get tired of looking at it.'

He rested his chin on top of her head. 'Did I tell you how much I love you?'

She smiled, a warm, generous curve widening her mouth. 'Not in the last few hours.'

'Or how beautiful you are?'

'A girl could get a swelled head,' she teased lightly, and felt his lips shift to nuzzle at the edge of her neck. Sensation shimmered through her body, heating her blood with need.

'I want to hold you, touch you,' he said gently as he swept an arm beneath her knees and lifted her against his chest. 'And never let you go.'

Heaven, she breathed with a sigh, was right here with him. Deep in her heart she knew it always would be.

'Sweet-talking me into bed, huh?' She linked her hands at his nape and pressed a string of kisses to the edge of his jaw.

'Do I need to?'

He reached the bedroom and gently released her to her feet.

'I'm yours,' Tasha vowed softly, pulling his head down to hers. 'Always.'

The kiss became an erotic, evocative imitation of the sexual act itself, satisfying to a degree, but not enough.

Her hands tugged the shirt free from his trousers as he reached for the hem of her top, and seconds later they caressed warm, silk-smooth skin, the touch of lips, hands brought forth a telling sigh, a husky groan in the prelude to a long, sweet loving lasting far into the night.

They rarely made it out of the apartment during their stay, and only left the bed to shower and eat.

Monday morning they rose soon after the dawn, showered, dressed, drove to Tedder Avenue, where they ate breakfast at one of several pavement cafés, then they joined the stream of traffic traversing the highway to Brisbane.

Jared drew the car into the pavement outside her office building and pressed a brief, hard kiss to her mouth.

'Have a good day.' His smile was something else, and she could have drowned in the wealth of emotion in his dark eyes. 'Take care.'

She trailed gentle fingers down his cheek. 'You too.'

His hand closed round her wrist and brought her

fingers to his lips, touching them to the ring he'd placed there only two days ago. 'Until tonight.'

She wanted to laugh and cry at the same time. 'Count on it.' Then she slid from the seat, closed the door, and stood watching as he eased the car into the traffic.

Life, she accorded in silent bemusement, didn't get any better than this.

EPILOGUE

SIOBHAN MARIE NORTH made her appearance into the world three days early via an emergency Caesarean section, and proved with ear-splitting velocity there was nothing wrong with her lungs…or anything else, thank you very much.

Her father was utterly captivated at first sight, treating her as something so infinitely precious he intended to fiercely defend with his dying breath.

Dark hair, delicate features, she resembled her mother in miniature, with an impatience to feed that hinted at a strong mind.

'Stubborn,' Jared teased gently.

'Determined,' Tasha corrected, and felt her heart melt at the depth of love evident as he watched mother and child.

His gaze lifted to meet hers, and the heat in it seared right through to her soul. 'How soon before you can come home?'

Her smile held a mischievous sparkle. 'Five or six days.'

They took Siobhan home on the sixth day to be greeted by a doting grandmother. Monica revelled in the role, and organised meals, household chores for a few weeks, and returned for the christening.

A year to the day when Tasha had first discovered

her pregnancy. The date had been a coincidental choice, and she wondered if Jared realised its significance.

Their daughter had been changed and fed, and was on the verge of sleep as her parents stood close by, arms entwined round each other's waist.

The nursery light had been dimmed, the baby intercom system switched on, and a sense of peace reigned.

'No regrets?' Tasha queried quietly.

'Not one.'

His incredulity meant more than the words.

'I'm glad.'

'Independence is a fine thing in a woman,' Jared said gently, lowering his head to brush his lips to hers. 'But you didn't stand a chance of it being anything other than temporary.'

A matter of weeks, she mused in retrospect, her flight from his apartment and their separation a vivid memory.

'She's asleep,' he confirmed softly, easing his wife from the room.

The christening had gone well, Siobhan was a model babe, and the small celebration for family and close friends had been a success.

Now Jared had a few plans of his own.

'I should go downstairs and—'

'No.'

'No?'

'I have something else in mind.'

'Such as?'

'The way I figure it, we have three hours before our daughter is due to wake.'

An impish bubble of laughter escaped her throat. 'And in those three hours you hope to achieve…?'

His hand slid down to cup her bottom, then traced her spine to settle at her nape. 'A leisurely love-making with my wife.'

'I think that could be arranged.'

'A little persuasion might help?'

Tasha turned in to him and pulled his head down to hers. 'Try me.'

He did. With such care, his degree of *tendresse* made her want to cry.

'I love you.' Words eloquently spoken in the aftermath of passion.

Words they both knew they'd repeat again and again in the years to follow as they travelled life's journey together. And beyond.

The world's bestselling romance series.

HARLEQUIN®
Presents

Seduction and Passion Guaranteed!

MISTRESS TO A MILLIONAIRE

She's his in the bedroom, but he can't buy her love...

The ultimate fantasy becomes a reality in Harlequin Presents®

Live the dream with more *Mistress to a Millionaire* titles by your favorite authors.

Coming in May
THE ITALIAN'S TROPHY MISTRESS
by Diana Hamilton #2321

Pick up a Harlequin Presents® novel and you will enter a world of spine-tingling passion and provocative, tantalizing romance!

Available wherever Harlequin Books are sold.

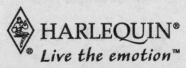

HARLEQUIN®
Live the emotion™

Visit us at www.eHarlequin.com

HPMTAMIL

A "Mother of the Year" contest brings
overwhelming response as thousands of women
vie for the luxurious grand prize....

Kate Hoffmann

Jacqueline Diamond

Jill Shalvis

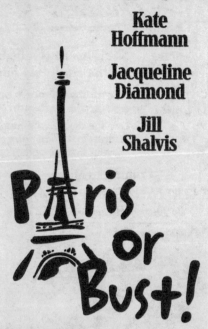

Paris or Bust!

A hilarious and romantic trio of new stories!

With a trip to Paris at stake, these women are
determined to win! But the laughs are many as three of
them discover that being finalists isn't the most
excitement they'll ever have.... Falling in love is!

Available in April 2003.

HARLEQUIN®

Makes any time special ®

Visit us at www.eHarlequin.com

PHPOB

Forgetting the past can destroy the future...

TARA TAYLOR
QUINN

AMANDA
STEVENS

Bring you two full-length novels of riveting romantic intrigue in...

YESTERDAY'S
MEMORIES

Two people struggle to regain their memories while rediscovering past loves, in this gripping volume of reading.

Look for it in May 2003— wherever books are sold.

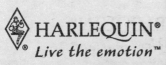

HARLEQUIN®
Live the emotion™

Visit us at www.eHarlequin.com

BR2YM

There's nothing sexier than a man in uniform...
so just imagine what three will be like!

MEN OF COURAGE

A brand-new anthology from
***USA TODAY* bestselling author**

LORI
FOSTER

DONNA KAUFFMAN   JILL SHALVIS

**These heroes are strong, fearless...
and absolutely impossible to resist!**

Look for MEN OF COURAGE in May 2003!

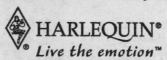

HARLEQUIN®
Live the emotion™

Visit us at www.eHarlequin.com

PHMOC

eHARLEQUIN.com

Sit back, relax and enhance your romance
with our great magazine reading!

- **Sex and Romance!** Like your romance
  hot? Then you'll *love* the sensual reading
  in this area.

- **Quizzes!** Curious about your lovestyle?
  His commitment to you? Get the
  answers here!

- **Romantic Guides and Features!**
  Unravel the mysteries of love with
  informative articles and advice!

- **Fun Games!** Play to your heart's content....

**Plus...romantic recipes,
top ten lists,
Lovescopes...and more!**

**Enjoy our online magazine today—
visit www.eHarlequin.com!**

INTMAG

"Georgette Heyer has given me great pleasure over the years
in my reading, and rereading, of her stories."
—#1 *New York Times* bestselling author Nora Roberts

Experience the wit, charm
and irresistible characters of

GEORGETTE
HEYER

creator of the modern Regency romance genre

Enjoy six new collector's editions with forewords
by some of today's bestselling romance authors:
**Catherine Coulter, Kay Hooper, Stella Cameron,
Diana Palmer, Stephanie Laurens and Linda Howard.**

The Grand Sophy
March

The Foundling
April

Arabella
May

The Black Moth
June

These Old Shades
July

Devil's Cub
August

Available at your favorite retail outlet.

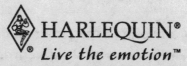

HARLEQUIN®
Live the emotion™

Visit us at www.eHarlequin.com

PHGH